MW00625862

MAGGIE OF CROSSWELL

Opal M. Snyder

Righter Books

Copyright 2013 by Opal May Snyder
All rights reserved
No part of this book may be reproduced without written permission by the author and by the publisher. This is a work of fiction. Any resemblance to actual persons or events is purely coincidental,

Righter Publishing Company, Inc.
410 River Oaks Parkway
Timberlake, North Carolina 27583

www.righterbooks.com

First Edition
January 2014

Printed and bound in the United States of America

Library of Congress Control Number
2014930426

Cover designed by Barbara Alston

ISBN 978-1-938527-23-4
Maggie of Crosswell
By Opal M. Snyder

Available on Amazon Kindle

Dedication

This book is dedicated to my editor, Peggy Ellis, for without her I could not have completed this book. *Maggie of Crosswell* is a fictional story written in my 95th year.

Thank you, Peggy

Opal M. Snyder
January 31, 2014

Chapter 1

Massive stone lions guarded the gates of the Crosswell School for Girls, formerly the majestic home of Judge Clarence Creighton Crosswell, Chief Judge of the Iowa Supreme Court, until his death in 1935. In his will, Judge Crosswell directed that the mansion be used as a school for abandoned girls, who could live there until they were 21. When the home was no longer used for a school, Judge Crosswell directed his heirs to sell the home and its surrounding ten acres.

Judge Crosswell had left an endowment fund of $500,000, the earnings from which was for maintenance of Crosswell. When the school reverted to the heirs, the endowment principal would be part of the estate.

The first and only Director of the school was Rachel Rebecca Cooper, who ruled for 42 years with an iron hand, tempered with kindness. She had been a tutor for Judge Crosswell's granddaughters, so the family asked her to run the school.

Miss Cooper was 30 years old when she began at Crosswell. Five foot eight, carrying herself in an almost regal manner, Miss Cooper prided herself that her weight was proportionate to her height. With the exception of Sunday mornings, when visiting ministers came to Crosswell, she wore navy or black tailored suits, topped with a white cotton blouse, which she ironed herself. On Sundays, she wore tea-length dresses, all made from fabric suitable to the season. In all her years at Crosswell, never once did she appear in front of the girls in casual wear, robe, or nightclothes.

Miss Cooper was fond of telling her pupils she was qualified to be director, principal, and teacher for all the grades through high school. "My degrees are in Secondary and Elementary Education, English Literature, and Accounting, which makes it possible for me to guide all of you," she recited each fall to her assembled charges. Secretly, she prided herself that most of her students ranked at the top of the Basic Skills test given each year.

There was a plan for every girl. Girls who were of a 'business bent' went to Capitol City high school and took typing, shorthand, and basic accounting. Girls of a 'scientific bent' studied chemistry and science, and did lab work. Those who 'didn't take to education' received training in cooking, housekeeping, sewing, and other skills. Miss Cooper placed them in private homes to 'learn how to get along in the world.'

Most of the girls left Crosswell well before they were 21, but all left prepared to earn a living. Many moved to Capitol City and found employment in stores or in offices. Miss Cooper did not approve of restaurant work for Crosswell girls. Each girl received a reference from Miss Cooper and lived at the YWCA until Miss Cooper found suitable housing for them.

Crosswell was admirably suited for conversion to a school for abandoned girls although she always described it as a school for young ladies. She never admitted children under five because she wanted her students to start learning 'life's lessons' at the kindergarten level.

There were seven large bedrooms, usually two girls to a room. The little girls were in a room with an older girl, who was responsible for seeing that the younger child was dressed and at the breakfast table promptly at seven every morning.

They attended morning devotions in the 'parlor' at 7:45 and lessons began at nine. Between devotions and the time lessons started, the girls made their beds and straightened their rooms. If the rooms passed inspection, the girls were permitted to walk in the front garden, down the winding driveway to the front gate and back. Many times, Miss Cooper accompanied the girls, sometimes she sent the resident housekeeper, Esther March, with them.

An architect had been engaged to convert a large music room into a classroom. One large wall was a blackboard, complete with the alphabet printed in uppercase and lowercase letters. A third row contained the alphabet in the Palmer method of handwriting. Miss Cooper's desk was at the front in the center of the room. A piano was in one corner of the room, and plants sat on large windowsills beneath the tall Victorian windows. The solid oak floor was polished to a shine.

The dining room at Crosswell was undisturbed from the way Judge Crosswell's family left it. A long table, which could seat 16, dominated the room. A mahogany 'to the ceiling' china cabinet held the dishes; the sideboard had lower drawers where tablecloths and silverware were stored. Miss Cooper presided at the meals and each girl, upon reaching the seventh grade, was required to ask the blessing.

Miss Cooper kept Judge Crosswell's office for her own. Here were the files for each girl and records of maintenance costs, grocery and clothing bills. Auditors always found the books 'kept to the penny'.

Because Miss Cooper believed in 'keeping up with the times', she purchased the most modern equipment: a state of the art calculator, electric typewriter and an intercom system, which came with two outside phone lines.

The front parlor served as the living room. Books lined the shelves and there was a record player, on which the girls played recordings of Miss Cooper's choosing, and a large television. Comfortable chairs and two old-fashioned lamps lent gentleness to the room. Miss Cooper firmly believed in the refinements of modern living so that her students could be at ease in any place they chose to live or work.

There was no dishwasher in the large kitchen because Miss Cooper believed that, when the girls married and had a home, few of them would be able to afford dishwashers. The stove was quite large as were the twin sinks. The kitchen floor was the original tile and there were two long counters where the girls learned food preparation. Cabinets lined three walls of the kitchen.

The laundry room, off the kitchen, boasted three electric washers and three dryers. Here the girls learned laundry techniques and were required to do their own laundry when they entered the seventh grade. Three ironing boards were left set up.

Miss Cooper accounted for every nail, every bar of soap, and every morsel of food. The county paid board and room to Crosswell for every girl committed by the court. Those funds made up about ninety percent of the budget, leaving most of the original endowment for maintenance, as the Judge directed.

Each summer there was a large garden all the girls helped with the harvest and canned food for the winter.

Miss Cooper also taught the girls sewing. Each fall and spring, she purchased yards of fabric and modern patterns. Upon entering the seventh grade, each girl completed a simple dress as part of her sewing instruction.

In the winter evenings, Miss Cooper gathered the girls in the parlor and read to them from the classics and the Bible. Promptly at 7:30, she held evening devotions, and at eight o'clock, the younger girls went to bed. The older girls were free to read, listen to music or play lady-like card games. They could also watch selected TV programs. The lights went out at ten.

At six each morning, Miss Cooper, after dressing and drinking a cup of strong black tea, went to her office where she worked on the Crosswell ledgers. She joined the girls for seven o'clock breakfast, and the day at Crosswell began.

It was into this ordered, predictable world of Crosswell, that Margaret Saville Monahan, age ten, arrived on June 30, 1965 at eleven in the morning accompanied by Rose Cherney, one of the county's social workers.

Chapter 2

Rose Cherney rang the doorbell of Crosswell, Maggie's hand held firmly in hers.

Miss Cooper answered the door.

"I've brought one of the Monahan children."

"Come in," Miss Cooper said and led the way to her office. She saw in a quick glance that the child's bare legs had a golden tan and the strap on one sandal was nearly loose from the shoe. Her too-short dress was badly faded and part of the lace on the sleeve was missing as well as one button on the front of the dress.

Maggie was almost lost in the big leather chair opposite Miss Cooper, who sat at Judge Crosswell's desk.

Rose Cherney started to talk, but Miss Cooper cut her off.

She smiled at Maggie. "What is your full name?"

Maggie looked Miss Cooper straight in the eye and answered, "Margaret Saville Monahan. My mama calls me Maggie."

Miss Cooper responded to this confidence, "Welcome to Crosswell, Margaret. Now when is your birthday and how old will you be?"

"September 25th and I'll be ten."

Miss Cooper pushed a button on her desk. Shortly, Esther March, the housekeeper, appeared, smoothing her white apron over a dark gray uniform.

Rose Cherney began to talk about Maggie as if the child were not there. "I expect her hair will be a real problem. Typical Irish—blue eyes and unruly hair that ..."

Miss Cooper interrupted her in mid-sentence. "Margaret and I will decide about her hair. She is now one of the Crosswell girls. Esther, please take Margaret to her room. She is to bathe and have an early lunch, then she is to rest. I will talk with her at one o'clock."

Without a word of protest, Maggie took Esther's outstretched hand and they left the room.

Rose, eager to spell out Maggie's background continued. "Soap and water and clean clothing will do wonders. Why the father persists in running off to find that mother I don't know ... and naming that child Margaret Saville ... she must have been reading trashy novels before the child was born. I hope you can do something with her, but you haven't much to work with. As you can see, her clothing is poorly washed and her hair must be cut!"

Ice tinged Miss Cooper's voice. "Miss Cherney, Margaret will be just fine. She is only the product of her environment. As you are well aware, she will learn all she needs to know at Crosswell to make her way in the world."

Miss Cherney was not convinced. "Well, I don't know. With such a mother ... do you realize that child's been alone in that shack of a house for five whole days? Then the neighbors alerted our office. The juvenile detention home is full, so Judge Stern ordered her to Crosswell as an abandoned child. Of course, the county will pay until her parents claim her, which I doubt will ever happen!"

Miss Cherney pulled a large manila envelope from her briefcase and handed it to Miss Cooper.

Taking the envelope from her, Miss Cooper stood up and ushered Rose to the front door. "I must supervise the preparation of the noon meal. Goodbye, Miss Cherney."

Miss Cooper did not go to the kitchen immediately, but sat at her desk, scanning the papers Rose had given her: three children, Maggie the youngest, last known address 2506 Front Street. Miss Cooper recalled the area near the outskirts of the west side of Capitol City ... small homes, shacks located near the railroad tracks a half block away. Maggie's history noted she was in the fourth grade. The teacher's commentary was that 'Maggie was bright enough and could succeed if given a chance, but there has never been an indication of parental interest. The two boys, 15 and 16, dropped out of high school and their whereabouts are unknown.'

Miss Cooper read the teacher's notation again: 'if given a chance'. It was at that moment that Rachel Rebecca Cooper decided that Margaret Saville Monahan would have a chance ... indeed, she would personally provide that chance.

Margaret, Miss Cooper told herself, will make her way in the world.

Then she opened the second desk drawer, laid the folder on top of the unfinished work, and went to the kitchen where two of the older girls were starting to prepare lunch.

***

Esther, the housekeeper, apologized to Miss Cooper. "I brushed her hair and combed it, but I can't get it to ..." she hesitated, remembering Miss Cooper's icy response to Rose Cherney ... "look neat."

"Perhaps Margaret would like to have Miss Foster style her hair when she comes on Thursday. Thank you, Esther. Margaret and I will visit for a while.

Esther left the room.

"Margaret, tell me about your family."

"My brothers went away. Then Mama went away. Then my daddy went to find her."

"Why do you think your mother left?" Miss Cooper's voice softened.

"I think Mama wants to go some place and be a singer. She sings real good. I don't think she wanted to stay home and take care of me. She plays the guitar, too. My daddy cries when she sings and then he drinks beer and then he cries some more and then he goes to sleep."

"Do you have relatives, aunts and uncles and cousins?"

"My cousin Lucy is ten, too. She lives in Texas. I have a picture of her. Miss Cherney said I could bring my box of things, but she didn't bring it."

"I'll call Miss Cherney to bring your things so you can have your cousin's picture on your dresser. Grace Perkins will room with you. She'll help you get acquainted. This afternoon, we'll go into Capitol City and I'll take you to Dr. Kaul. This will be just a regular

14

checkup. Then, if there's time, we'll go over to Parker's Department Store and get you three dresses. You'll need one to wear, one for spare, and one in the laundry. Now, tell me about church, Margaret. Did your parents take you to a special one?"

"No. Mama never went to church, but she sings church songs about Jesus. I'm good at school. I like to read and I'm practicing cursive. I can't spell too good, but I can do my arithmetic!" Maggie's eyes shone after imparting this bit of her past.

"I'm glad you like school, Margaret. I am the teacher here at Crosswell, and I will help you with your spelling."

Miss Cooper buzzed again for Esther, who came immediately. "Take Margaret to the parlor, please, and show her where the books are. She can read a little and then I'll drive her into the city for her physical and pick up a few items for her. The girls will need to meet in the parlor at five so that Margaret can meet them."

Miss Cooper dialed the doctor's office and was fortunate to learn he had a cancellation for a 3:30 appointment.

They arrived 15 minutes ahead of time. Maggie dangled her feet from the chair in the waiting room and stared around the room.

After checking her ears, eyes, and throat and listening to her heart and lungs, Dr. Kaul declared Maggie to be in good health. "She's a little underweight, Miss Cooper, but you'll soon fix that. She has two cavities, which you'll want taken care of ... and let's give this young lady some vitamins for a month or two. I expect her medical records will come.

"Certainly, Doctor, whatever I receive from Social Services I'll forward to your office immediately."

Dr. Kaul opened the door of the examining room into the hallway and gave Maggie two small sample bottles of vitamin pills.

"Bring her back in six months, Miss Cooper, and we'll see how she's getting along. Goodbye, Margaret." He smiled at her as she left the office holding Miss Cooper's hand.

They drove to Parker's Department Store. From long habit, Miss Cooper went directly to the Girls' Department and picked out three dresses. Then she purchased seven pairs of underpants, a package of anklets, three slips and two nightgowns. "Do you like the dresses, Margaret?"

"They're pretty. Do I get to keep them?"

"Of course, you do. Now let's see about some shoes to finish the summer." Miss Cooper selected sturdy tennis shoes and a pair of plain patent leather shoes for Sunday. Maggie seemed pleased and asked if she could put her old ones in the shoebox. Miss Cooper signed the sales slips to be charged to Crosswell and they left the store and drove back to Crosswell in the school's Pontiac station wagon.

On the way to Crosswell, Maggie again asked Miss Cooper if she could get her box of things.

"Yes, Margaret, I'll call Miss Cherney when we get back to Crosswell and you can keep your things in your dresser. I'll make an appointment with Dr.

Barton, the dentist, and you'll be ready to begin school this fall. If you study hard, Margaret, you will be prepared to go into the world and earn your living when you are older. Knowledge is power, Margaret. Always remember that. When you have knowledge, you can be anything you want to be."

"Can I be a singer like Mama?"

"I don't know right now, Margaret. First, you must have an education. Then you need to have others help you to determine if you have singing talent. Probably you will need someone in the music world to manage a singing career. However, first, you must have an education. That is the first step. You need to learn how to manage money to pay for things you need and want."

"Sometimes Daddy didn't have the rent money and we had to move."

"That happens when there's not enough money to pay for what a family needs, Margaret."

"Can I learn how to do something so I can always pay my rent and won't be hungry? Sometimes, we didn't have enough money and I was hungry."

"Indeed you will, Margaret. If your parents do not come to take you home again, and you stay at Crosswell until you finish high school, you will be able to earn enough to pay for your food and rent. Above all, you must save some money from every paycheck. Pay yourself first, Margaret. That is how you prepare for the future."

"I don't think Mama will come for me. I don't know where Kenny and Joey are either. I think I'm going to stay at Crosswell a long time."

"Perhaps you will, Margaret."

The girls were assembled in the parlor when Miss Cooper and Maggie arrived.

Chapter 3

It seemed to Maggie that the years passed quickly. She never forgot her mother, but Miss Cooper quickly became the important adult in Maggie's life. She worked hard and strived to please the woman who was always there to deal with Maggie's adolescent problems.

In the intervening years between the time Maggie came to Crosswell and when Miss Cooper went to London in 1977, Maggie had completed her education at Midland University with a major in Elementary Education and a Minor in Accounting. She had also completed personnel and specialized courses in business management during the summer months, all this with Miss Cooper's encouragement.

It had long been Miss Cooper's plan to groom Maggie to take over Crosswell when she retired, but neither of them knew that Judge Crosswell's heirs would elect to sell the property for a housing development within the next two years. Maggie also didn't know that Miss Cooper had changed the plan for her life work. For that matter, Miss Cooper did not know she would never live to see her new plan for Margaret completed.

Rachel Cooper's death was as swift as she would have planned it, should any mortal have the chance. There was no lingering in a nursing home, no wheelchair, no bedfast days. A car hit her as she crossed a London street and she died instantly.

* * *

Maggie learned of Miss Cooper's death on a Monday morning early in May. She was the acting director at Crosswell and occupied with paperwork at the desk where Miss Cooper first interviewed her.

The telephone interrupted the mundane tasks of writing menus and assigning chores. It was Anthony Dawson, Miss Cooper's attorney. His voice was flat, utterly devoid of emotion, as if he were talking about a stranger even though Rachel Cooper had been his client all of her adult life.

"Miss Monahan, I'm sorry to inform you that Miss Cooper died in an automobile accident while traveling in London. I will be at Crosswell at one o'clock to inform the girls. Miss Cherney will accompany me. I would prefer you let me tell them. Miss Cherney has assured me she will assist the girls in settling at the YWCA until they find suitable housing. The two girls still in high school will complete their education and Miss Cherney will assist them, perhaps in a board and room arrangement in exchange for light housekeeping duties. The Crosswell heirs have decided to sell the property. They will put it on the market within a month."

* * *

Anthony Dawson greeted each girl by name, after carefully reading the 3 x 5 cards Maggie had prepared. There were no little girls left at Crosswell. Only seven girls remained, two of whom were in high school and five who were working in the community but living at Crosswell.

Dawson told the girls that Miss Cooper had died

in an automobile accident and that Miss Cherney would find housing for them elsewhere. "Please sign the cards for the flowers, girls. Burial will be in Memorial Garden."

Maggie dismissed the girls and, as each one stood to go, Dawson shook her hand and wished her well. Rose Cherney again assured the girls she would help them get settled in a new home.

After the girls and Miss Cherney left the room, Dawson said to Maggie, "I will read Miss Cooper's will on Friday morning. Can you arrange to be in my office at nine? I believe you are to use the station wagon."

Automatically, Maggie pulled out a narrow lined pad from her pocket and began to take notes. "Yes, Mr. Dawson, I'll be there. Will I remain at Crosswell until it is sold?"

"I don't think so, but Miss Cooper left detailed plans for you with me before she left for London. She planned to close Crosswell when she returned and turn the property back to the heirs. I would advise you to do nothing until you hear Miss Cooper's will, but I can assure you that Miss Cooper has provided direction for you and there is no need for you to find housing. Miss Cherney will not need to assist you." Dawson closed the door of Crosswell behind him and returned to the city.

* * *

The Reverend Potter Palmer conducted Miss Cooper's funeral at the Magnolia Street Methodist Church. The casket was closed.

21

There were no relatives left to honor Miss Cooper's long and useful life, but her 'family' from Crosswell, the seven remaining girls, Esther the housekeeper, along with Maggie, occupied the two front pews of the sanctuary. Other girls who owed so much to Rachel Cooper over the years occupied several pews. Miss Cherney was late.

Many of the teachers from the community attended, as did Anthony Dawson and the president of the Magnolia Trust and Savings Bank, Curtis J. Charlesworth.

As the service got underway, Maggie remembered that 'How Great Thou Art' was Miss Cooper's favorite hymn. She listened to the familiar passages from the Psalms that all the Crosswell girls had committed to memory. The Reverend Potter gave a brief biography of Miss Cooper, including her years at Crosswell. He timed it well. Exactly 30 minutes from the time the organist started the prelude, the service was over.

Only Maggie, Esther and Mr. Dawson went to the cemetery. Maggie, for the first time since coming to Crosswell, felt utterly alone as the workers lowered the casket into the earth.

After the funeral, Dawson's parting words to Maggie were, "See you Friday at nine. Again, may I tell you how sorry I am at Miss Cooper's sudden passing?"

***

Maggie shut the door to the station wagon and walked into her bedroom at Crosswell. She sat on the only chair, methodically pulled off her gloves, put her hat in its box, and then lay across her bed and cried for Miss Cooper, the only true friend in the 22 years of her life.

The next morning, Miss Cherney helped the girls get their things together. She promised that, if the furnishings at Crosswell were to be sold, she would come back for a day or two and help Maggie get ready for the sale. Miss Cherney paused as she turned toward the door. "Are you afraid to stay alone, Margaret? I could ask one of the girls to stay with you."

"No, Miss Cherney, but thank you."

Maggie kissed girls on the cheek, as Miss Cooper would have done, and told them goodbye. She stood at the front door as the girls piled into Miss Cherney's van and waved goodbye.

She shut the door and then walked through the quiet rooms, sensing Miss Cooper's presence. Everything was in order. The chairs in the parlor were ready for the 'quiet hour'. In the downstairs bathroom, Maggie opened a large cupboard. The towels were neatly stacked in units of three … one bath, one hand, and one washcloth. Toilet tissue, shampoo, soap and toothpaste were neatly stacked on the upper shelves. She wondered what would happen to the supplies. The tiled floor smelled faintly of bleach. Maggie dampened a tissue from the container on the counter and wiped a fingerprint smudge from the mirror.

Maggie stopped when she reached Miss Cooper's office. The desk contained receipts and correspondence from the last five years of Crosswell's operation. There were receipts for utility bills, grocery bills, clothing bills for the girls, bank statements along with bills from people who kept up the grounds. In another divided section of the drawer there were folders marked 'Personnel at Crosswell'. Maggie found hers. On a blank page, she saw words that took her back to her first day here: Great potential. There was nothing more. Maggie glanced through the files of the seven girls in her charge. Mary Katherine Phillips, her birthdate, mumps when she was 12, poor speller, must be encouraged to finish work assigned. The others had similar notations after their names.

Maggie found nothing more about herself. She opened the center drawer. The checkbook, balanced the day before Miss Cooper left, showed a balance of $17,425.75. Miss Cooper's pen was the only one in the small grooved compartment. A desk calendar with nothing filled in beyond the day Miss Cooper left for her trip, stood mutely on the top of the desk. There was one exception. On the 15th of August, a week after Miss Cooper would have arrived home, was the notation, 'see Dawson'.

None of Miss Cooper's personal belongings remained at Crosswell. Sometime before the trip, Maggie never knew when, Miss Cooper had moved her things to her own home, a recently built duplex whose address was Box 27, 934 West Lombard Avenue, Davenport, Iowa. Maggie had never been there.

As she sat alone at Miss Cooper's desk, the Judge's desk, as Miss Cooper was fond of saying,

Margaret Saville Monahan did not know she would be the new owner of Miss Cooper's duplex on Lombard Street, five miles from the Capitol City Office building where she would meet Anthony Dawson on Friday.

She only knew that she had never felt so alone in her life.

Chapter 4

Maggie dressed carefully for the READING, which she thought of in uppercase because it apparently contained something about her life, right now in limbo. She stood at the front hall mirror for a long time checking the details of her outfit. She chose a black suit, about three inches below her knee and a blouse, which had tiny pearl buttons marching down the front, starting at the mandarin collar. The black mid-heel shoes were new that spring, and Miss Cooper had given her a black leather handbag for Christmas.

She could almost hear Miss Cooper's advice ... *when dressing for business, Margaret, wear dark, modest length dresses with a little white at the collar. A business suit with a white tailored blouse is appropriate. A small unobtrusive pin is permissible, no runs in your hose, shoes well shined and always, Margaret, always, wear gloves. Your handbag should be neatly arranged, your small lined pad and pen ever ready to record directions ... keep your hair neat ... pin it back while you are working. Always, always, without fail, change underclothing every day. Use perfume sparingly, if at all, and no painted nails, no painted face. Naturalness, Margaret, is much more attractive than paint.*

The speech about how to dress, one of many, was the first one Maggie learned to transcribe from her shorthand notes.

Tucking a tendril behind her ear, Maggie wondered where she got her almost coal black hair.

Her mother had been a redhead and her father had sandy colored hair, which curled when it got too long. Her eyes were typical Irish blue and her skin so fair she spent little time in the sun since leaving childhood.

Again, Miss Cooper's voice came unbidden to her thoughts: *It is not necessary to look dowdy, but one should always feel at ease. If clothing is too short, one is always fussing with the skirt, pulling it down when sitting.*

Maggie was sure her mentor would have given approval. She picked up the car keys from the table by the door and calmly drove to Anthony Dawson's office to hear Miss Cooper's will.

Mr. Dawson greeted Maggie with a solemn 'good morning' and motioned her to the deep leather chair in front of his desk. He sat down in an identical chair opposite her and handed her a copy of 'The Last Will and Testament of Rachel Rebecca Cooper'.

He began to read. The first paragraph was standard: 'I, Rachel Rebecca Cooper, a resident of Davenport, Iowa, do hereby make, publish and declare this to be my last will and testament, hereby revoking all former wills and codicils written by me'.

Article 1 stated 'I nominate my attorney, Anthony Dawson, to be my executor and trustee and carry out the terms of this will according to the probate laws of the State of Iowa. He shall give an accounting to my ward, Margaret Saville Monahan, on a regular basis'.

Article 2 dealt with expenses, debts and taxes to be paid by the estate.

Article 3 spelled out Miss Cooper's plan for Maggie's career. 'I hereby give and bequeath my residual estate to my ward, Margaret Saville Monahan. This includes my checking account, savings, investments including five hundred thousand dollars in stocks and bonds, time certificates, and savings, my home on Lombard Street with its furnishings, and my 1975 Buick. I direct that investments be held in trust until the said Margaret Saville Monahan reaches age 25. Until she reaches age 25, all income from investments shall be credited to her checking account to invest and to spend, as she desires'.

Article 4 covered her plans for her ward. 'It is my fondest wish and hope that Margaret Saville Monahan will have a banking career, for therein lies the secret of independence for her. Specifically, it is my desire that my ward seek employment at the Magnolia Bank and Trust Company in the Trust Department. My estate is to pay her salary for one year to reimburse the bank for her training.'

The signature was in Rachel Cooper's distinctive Palmer Method of Handwriting. Two teaching associates signed as witnesses as well as a Notary Public. Miss Cooper believed in leaving nothing to chance.

Dawson broke Maggie's stunned silence. "Are there any questions, Miss Monahan?"

She could not take in the magnificence of her inheritance, so she said the only thing that came to mind. "But I don't know anything about banking. I have no education in that field. I only know institutional accounting. Do you know why Miss Cooper chose banking? She hinted some time ago that I would take over Crosswell!"

Dawson did not hesitate. "Crosswell will be sold. Sometime between when you finished your university education and when Miss Cooper learned of the pending sale, she changed her mind about your career plans. I think the will answers your questions. Independence. Do you recall a conversation many years ago when you and Miss Cooper talked about how education would prepare you to earn a living?"

"She always talked to all of us about the importance of an education, but in the last year, she talked about it even more."

"As I mentioned, sometime in the last year, she changed her mind about your future. She may have seen Crosswell as a dead end street for you and it turns out she was right."

"But Crosswell was her whole life. She loved the school. She often spoke to me in terms of 'when you take over Crosswell'!"

"Perhaps that is the clue, Miss Monahan. Crosswell was her whole life, and for some reason she changed her mind about it being your whole life."

Maggie was on the verge of tears, but finally managed to find words she needed to say. "She must have loved me to leave me everything. When did I become her ward?"

"When you were about 12, she became your guardian. As you are aware, your parents never contacted the court nor came to Crosswell to visit you.

Your brothers have never contacted you either, nor did anyone else."

He hesitated, then continued. "I think it best for you to keep your holdings private for a while. It will be a big adjustment for you to work outside Crosswell and being on your own without Miss Cooper to guide you."

Maggie nodded. She didn't even want to think about Miss Cooper not being there.

"Now, we will discuss your finances. I will transfer the balance of Miss Cooper's personal checking account to a checking account in your name immediately. I alerted the bank that you will be in to sign necessary documents and the bank will set up checking and savings accounts for you. I will call the bank today and advise their customer service department to expect you tomorrow, if that is satisfactory."

Maggie nodded again. Speech was beyond her.

"Here are the keys to the Lombard Street house. The utilities are already in your name. I believe it is best for you to move your personal belongings there, lock up Crosswell, and bring the keys to my office and leave them with my secretary on Monday morning. I will handle affairs for the Crosswell heirs. Should you need my advice about anything, please do not hesitate to call. As executor, until everything is settled regarding Miss Cooper's will and Crosswell, I remain your attorney as well as Crosswell's attorney."

Still overcome with the magnitude of the change in her life, Maggie mumbled an incoherent 'thank you' and started toward the door.

"Wait just a moment, Miss Monahan. I have a letter Miss Cooper left for you in the event of her unexpected death." Dawson's eyes were kind. "It's best to read it this evening when you're settled."

He shook hands with Maggie and held open the door for her.

She thanked him again. She hoped she would never have to call him, but at this moment, she couldn't begin to understand the ramifications of her inheritance.

Chapter 5

Maggie's mind was in a whirlwind of self-doubt as she drove to Crosswell for the last time. She slowed and paused to look fondly at the stone lions, the closest to a real pet of her own she'd ever had. There was a lump in her throat when she opened the door and gently laid the car keys on the small Queen Ann table in the foyer.

It took her less than a half hour to pack her few possessions. The furniture in her room belonged to Crosswell. She packed her books in boxes and carried out her clothes on hangers. She put her things from the dresser drawer in shopping bags she found in the laundry room. There was plenty of room in the Buick.

Maggie locked the front door and paused, again, at the gate where the lions held their lonely vigil. She blinked back her tears. This had been home for so long that she barely remembered living anywhere else. Or perhaps, she had blocked much of her early childhood from her mind in an effort to deal with her heartache over her family's neglect. She had rarely allowed herself to remember those days in the house alone after her father left, the days when she didn't have food and cried herself to sleep every night wondering what would happen to her. She had never told anyone about that, not even Miss Cooper.

She checked her purse again to be sure Miss Cooper's letter was still in it, then she drove to her new home on Lombard Street in Davenport. She didn't know what to expect, and was pleasantly surprised when she arrived. It was a duplex, about two years old. She noted the outside windows glistened in the afternoon sunrays. The door opened silently with the turn of the key Mr. Dawson had given to her.

A lamp, controlled by a sensor, lit the front hallway. Maggie glanced into the ground floor rooms, then went up the stairs, which led to the bedrooms. She paused a moment in the doorway to each of the two spare rooms, then approached the master suite, obviously the one Miss Cooper used. She swallowed a sob. Her brain rebelled at the thought of using Miss Cooper's things, including her bed, but she decided she might feel closer to her mentor if she did. She resolutely stepped inside. She placed the letter from Miss Cooper on a small desk in the corner of the room and set her purse on the closet shelf. She took a steadying breath as she pulled out the desk chair and opened the letter.

The date at the top of the page was June 1, 1977, the day before Miss Cooper left for her vacation in England. Maggie resisted reading the letter while she remembered the many times Miss Cooper had discussed the trip, which was a lifelong dream. She had chosen a trip that included seeing many of the sights made famous in English literature as well as places of historical interest. Maggie had loved hearing Miss Cooper's enthusiastic details.

Maggie finally nerved herself to read her mentor's final words to her.

My dear Margaret. Maggie winced as she remembered Miss Cooper had never called her

Maggie, although from time to time Maggie had hinted she would like to be called the name her mother had called her. However, Miss Cooper had frowned on nicknames for anyone, and continued to call her Margaret. Maggie returned her attention to the letter. She could almost hear the beloved voice.

I think it is best for you not to pursue a career in private school education, but in the field of banking. You have a sharp mind and I have no doubt you will grasp the rudiments of the banking world quickly. I would like you to begin your career at Magnolia Trust and Savings Bank and work there one year. My estate will pay for your training. Remember, you are going into the bank with a degree. You need only to learn about banking, which is like any other discipline; there are rules governing the banking business. I want you to learn how to make your money grow to provide for your entire life, no matter where life's pathway may take you.

Maggie blinked away some tears. She couldn't even begin to fathom what life held for her.

You are a beautiful young woman and I reared you to be a lady. Perhaps you will marry someday and have children. If that is your wish, although to marry was not mine, I will be happy for you. I chose to live as a single person. To marry, or not, is a matter of personal choice. Trust in God and in yourself and you will be happy, although you will encounter disappointment and heartache from time to time. You have inner strength, Margaret. I knew from the moment Rose Cherney brought you into my office when you were a child of ten, that, with some guidance, you would make your way in the world. Count Anthony Dawson as a friend, and do not hesitate to call on him, should the need arise.

About your wardrobe, Margaret. Buy something new each season so that your peers will respect you. Also, this way you will keep up with the times.

Take a few evening courses to help you with your work at the bank, and call on the bank's president, Mr. Charlesworth, for help in that regard. He's my second cousin.

I hope you will affiliate with a church and find friends there.

Maggie realized that she had no friends now that Crosswell was not part of her life. Her friends from her school days had scattered.

Now, about the tenant in your house. Mr. Lawrence Scott has resided in the other half of your duplex since the beginning and my arrangements with him included his taking care of the lawn, shoveling snow, and washing the outside windows. This he will continue to do. He has faithfully kept his part of our rental agreement. He makes his rent payment directly to the bank, which will credit it to your account. You will find Mr. Scott reserved. He teaches philosophy at the Huntingford Campus of the university. It is not necessary for you to socialize with him, but you can count on him to offer any assistance you might need.

I don't need to remind you to keep records for tax purposes and for the maintenance of the property, which will appreciate in value, should you wish to sell it sometime in the future.

You were as dear to me as any daughter could have been and you have been God's blessing to me.

I leave you with regret, but in God's hands.

Maggie lowered her face into her hands and sobbed. She'd never considered herself a blessing to anyone. Far from it, in fact. If her own family couldn't love her, why would anyone else? But Miss Cooper did. How could she go on without this woman who had meant the world to her?

Chapter 6

The Magnolia Trust and Savings Bank was an imposing structure on the corner of Magnolia and Second Street in downtown Davenport, Iowa. Built in the early thirties, the building reflected the owner's fondness for Roman columns. The glass revolving doors sparkled as Maggie went in and stopped at a large desk in the front of the bank where a small, engraved sign said 'Information'. The young woman at the desk asked if she could help.

Mindful of Miss Cooper's oft-repeated admonition to be professional, Maggie used her formal name and produced an appointment card. "I'm Margaret Monahan, from Crosswell. I'm here to see Mr. Charlesworth. Anthony Dawson sent me."

The desk clerk directed her to the second floor. Maggie's welcome was not as friendly as she'd received downstairs. Mr. Charlesworth's secretary seemed irritated that anyone would bother her when she was working on her end-of-the-month report.

"Do you have an appointment?"

"I'm not sure. Mr. Dawson sent me. I'm from Crosswell."

"Crosswell?"

"Yes. I believe that Mr. Charlesworth is aware of my employment with the bank."

"Mr. Charlesworth won't be in today. Why don't you go down to the lower level and fill out an application at the personnel office? I'm sure they can help you. The elevator is to the left."

Maggie started to explain about Miss Cooper's will, but Mr. Charlesworth's secretary had turned to her calculator and started to add columns of figures from a yellow columnar pad. Maggie found the elevator and the personnel office to the right of the elevator in the basement. The office was a depressing green and was sparsely furnished compared to other areas of the bank. Maggie waited a few minutes until a young woman came and stood behind a tiled counter.

"Hi, I'm Catherine Tanner, Mr. Walker's assistant. Just fill out this application and Mr. Walker will be with you in a few minutes."

Maggie filled out the standard application form: her education, place of residence, past work experience, and hobbies, if any.

Back in his office, Lee Walker gripped the phone while he talked with Jared Holmes, the office administrator at Huntingford General Hospital.

"Look, Jared, I know you need to have someone in Medical Records that's got brain one. I'd like to help you out, but I can't afford to train secretaries and send them over there to you."

"You haven't sent anyone over here."

"How about that Jean somebody?"

"She applied here and we offered her more money."

"I just got her trained and she was doing a bang up job and you lured her away. I could name two or three people who have gone to your hospital from the bank."

"Well, why don't you pay more, then? Do you

have any applicants at all? My records supervisor is threatening to quit if I don't get her some help in the files."

At that moment, Catherine Tanner tossed Maggie's application onto Walker's desk.

"Hold on, here's one of those Crosswell girls looking for work. Has a great handwriting ... went to college, too. I may be able to help you out this time. Don't pay her top scale or she won't come back to the bank. Send her back to the bank and we'll start her in our records. You owe me big time, Jared. I hope you realize that."

Walker hung up the phone and called out to Catherine: "Send Monahan in."

He wasted no time. "Well, Miss Monahan, we're going to send you over to the hospital to help out. They're changing their files and need someone for a short time to give them a hand. You'll be paid the same starting wage as in the bank and when you've finished their files you come on back to the bank and work for us."

Before Maggie could say a word, Walker rose from his desk and waved her out the door.

"I know I'll get good reports about you. All the Crosswell girls have excellent training. Goodbye, Miss Monahan."

Maggie went directly to the hospital and asked to see Mr. Holmes as Mr. Walker had instructed.

Holmes, a recent graduate in administration from the university and a longtime buddy of Walker's, greeted her heartily. "We're so glad you considered working for us and helping out, Miss Monahan. Let me introduce you to Miss Gallaway, who is supervisor of records."

He and Maggie walked from his office down a gleaming corridor and entered a large room where there were stacks of files on the floor with new boxes of file folders on a long table. An electric typewriter was on another table. There were rows of wooden shelving on the walls.

"Bertha," Holmes called out, "Look what I brought you. A real live helper. Went to college, too. When the files are done, she has to go back to the bank."

Bertha stood by her desk, which stood in one corner of the room, all the time Holmes was talking to her. She was a plump woman with gray hair pulled into a bun. She wore a black pants suit with a white blouse and kept adjusting her glasses. She had been with Medical Records for 20 years.

Holmes introduced them. "Margaret Monahan, Bertha Gallaway."

With that, Holmes left the room and Maggie and Bertha smiled at each other.

Bertha wasted no time. "I'm glad you're here. You can't believe the dumbbells they send me from the employment office. Half of them don't know the alphabet and pick out the letters on the typewriter with one finger. I threatened to quit if Holmes didn't get me some decent help."

Maggie smiled. "Well, I do know the alphabet and I type about 100 words a minute, and I take shorthand."

"Shorthand?"

"Yes."

"Don't breathe that to anyone. I'd lose you in a minute to transcription. You can put your purse in this closet. I'll get you a lunch ticket. The meals are at cost, and Payroll will deduct it from your paycheck. In the meantime, Margaret, start with this pile."

"Oh, do call me Maggie." No one other than Miss Cooper had ever called her Margaret.

"Okay, Maggie." Bertha motioned to the first pile of folders. "Here's a roll of labels. File the pages according to color. Each color signifies a different procedure, such as X-ray, surgery, medications and diagnosis all for the same patient. Then start filing the revised files in the file boxes and put the box on the shelving next to the window. When the phone rings, answer with 'Medical Records' and tell whoever it is that I'll be back shortly and take a message, if they wish to leave one."

Bertha went through the swinging doors, and Maggie inserted the roll of labels in the machine, picked up a stack of files and began her first day of work at Huntingford General.

Neither Mr. Dawson, her lawyer, nor Mr. Charlesworth, president of the bank, had any idea that Maggie Monahan was tucked away in Medical Records at Huntingford General and was not starting a career in banking.

Chapter 7

Maggie found her job at Huntingford General relaxing after the sudden upheaval in her life. She worked out a system where she took ten files, placed each file sheet in color-coded sequence as directed, tossed the old file folder into the wastebasket and placed the papers in a new folder. When ten folders were finished, she rechecked the spelling of each patient's name and doctor and made a new label, then placed it in the empty box. When the box was full, she made a new label for the box according to the alphabet.

Maggie soon learned Bertha's schedule. She went out for coffee shortly after nine and would return around eleven-thirty or so and work on papers on her desk and file new records as they came in. In the afternoon, she would leave her office for a couple of hours and return with reports for which she was responsible.

After Maggie had been at Huntingford for two weeks, a man wearing a rumpled lab coat and holding a tape in his hand interrupted her.

"Hi! I'm Dr. Allen, staff pathologist. Are you Bertha's new assistant?"

A *doctor*? Maggie took a deep breath. Time to be professional. "Yes. I'm Margaret Monahan."

"You must be pretty good. She's around the hospital a lot more than she used to be. She used to help me out once in a while when I needed something done in a hurry, when Transcription was on overload.

Look, I need this done, with four copies, for a three o'clock meeting. I've spelled out the medical terms."

"I'd be happy to help you, but are you sure it will be all right with Bertha?"

"Sure. I'll clear it with her. She owes me a favor anyhow. Here's the green sheet containing the typed path report. Could you buzz me when you're finished?"

"Certainly, Dr. Allen. Don't forget to tell Bertha, please."

Maggie found typing the path report a relaxing change from filing. Dr. Allen's voice was distinct. He had spelled out the medical terms, even added the commas and periods in the manuscript. She finished the report in 20 minutes. There were no errors. She found the doctor's extension number in Bertha's in-house directory.

"Dr. Allen, this is Margaret Monahan in Medical Records. Your report is ready. I think it best if I don't leave my office to go to the copy machine. Perhaps another time I could get your copies."

He appeared almost immediately. "Wow! I'd better call you Speedy Margaret. Or may I call you Maggie?" He turned toward the door without waiting for her answer. "This is great. I'll get the copies myself. Thanks a lot. I take it you're Irish with a name like Monahan!"

Maggie laughed and hoisted the next box of files from the floor onto the table. She began to dread the day she would leave the cozy office of Medical Records and start at the bank. She was in no hurry and began to look forward to the periods when Bertha would leave the office and she was by herself.

Three weeks after she typed the pathology report for Dr. Allen, he burst into Medical Records swearing. "That damn transcribing machine is on the fritz again and the secretaries are typing from hand notes. They're typing like crazy and here I am with no typist."

Maggie looked up from the Miller file. "What do you need, Dr. Allen?"

"I need this report on Mr. Jarvis' condition typed for a four o'clock meeting. I got the results of the test this morning. Doctors hate to take notes. We want it all written out for us. But look, if I dictate slowly from my handwritten notes, could you type it if I spelled out the medical terms? I could write it in longhand, but I doubt if you could read my handwriting."

"That won't be necessary Dr. Allen. I take shorthand. If you spell out the technical terms, you need only to dictate from your notes and I'll transcribe them."

"You take shorthand?"

"Yes."

"Why are you working on files? You're a crack typist. I didn't find one error in the other manuscript. I like the way you laid it out, too."

"I'm on loan to the hospital from Magnolia Trust and Savings. When I'm finished with these files, I'll go back to the bank. I think they will start me in Records, also."

Then Maggie smiled, opened her purse for a small lined notebook she always carried, thought of Miss Cooper, and asked Dr. Allen to begin.

He watched her as she inserted the green paper into her typewriter. "Could I just wait at Bertha's desk? I have a couple of calls to make. I promise I won't interrupt you. I'll answer Bertha's phone, too."

When he finished his calls, Dr. Allen studied Maggie.

That day, she was wearing her hair in a bun at the nape of her neck. She wore only a trace of lipstick and clear fingernail polish. The white blouse skimmed her figure with a black skirt falling midway between her knees and her ankles. Her shoes were sturdy, almost an oxford.

Maggie typed with a rhythm of one who has practiced a lot. When she finished the second page, she read the material rapidly, beginning with the right side of the page and reading to the left of each line, so she could catch any errors. When she finished, she stood up by the table and called to Dr. Allen.

"Dr. Allen, I've finished. Your report is ready."

He walked toward her, holding out his hand for the report. He was surprised to find that she was taller than he had remembered and that her long lashes framed incredibly blue eyes.

While he was talking to Maggie, Bertha walked into her office and greeted the doctor.

"Hi, Dr. Allen, what brings you down here in the bowels of the building?"

"Well, I borrowed Miss Monahan. Did you

know she takes shorthand and types all this stuff without errors? She's fast, too. What the hell is she doing in Records? Why isn't she somebody's private secretary?"

Bertha put her fingers to her lips. "That's our secret. You have to promise me you won't tell anyone she takes shorthand or else Personnel will take her away from both of us. Look at the great job she's doing on my files! When she gets caught up, I don't know what I'll have her do. Maybe she can work for both of us. We'll just share a secretary. You and me and, maybe, Pharmacy. He's always yelling he doesn't have time to do paperwork."

Dr. Allen paused on his way out the door, the sheaf of green paper in his hand. "Thanks a lot, Miss Monahan. Bertha, you be here tomorrow at ten sharp, because I'm taking Miss Monahan to coffee. Okay? ... And I promise ... not a word to anyone that she takes shorthand."

He left the room and Maggie finished the Miller file. Bertha went to her desk and dialed Jack Edwards, chief pharmacist at Huntingford General.

Chapter 8

The hospital's cafeteria was a sunny yellow with robin's egg blue accents. The chairs' vinyl covers were the same blue.

On a Friday morning, Dr. Allen stopped at the door of Medical Records. Bertha was at her desk and looked up, then motioned for Maggie to leave for her coffee break.

"She can have 15 minutes with you, Dr. Allen. She never takes breaks. You don't even drink coffee, do you, Maggie?"

"No, but I like tea."

"Well, fine," Dr. Allen said, taking Maggie's arm as they walked to the cafeteria. The coffee and tea were on a large table with cups stacked neatly beside the urns.

Maggie poured her tea.

"Sugar's over there," Dr. Allen said as he took a chair opposite Maggie.

"No sugar, thanks."

Dr. Allen began. "Now tell me all about how you are supposed to be at the bank and instead you're working here."

"Well, I'm a graduate of Crosswell and Midland University. My degree is in Elementary Education with a minor in Accounting."

Dr. Allen interrupted. "Why aren't you teaching? Or in an accounting position?"

Maggie sipped her tea, deciding how much to tell him. "Miss Cooper, my guardian and the head of

Crosswell, wanted me to run Crosswell when she retired, but then she changed her mind and decided I should have a career in banking." Maggie took a steadying breath. She didn't want to mention this, but felt she must. "Miss Cooper died on a trip to London. That's when I learned what she wanted me to do."

"Didn't you have a voice in the matter?"

"Not in the banking matter, but taking her place at Crosswell—we talked about that a lot. I didn't know anything about the banking part until I saw her will."

"What arrangements were made for you at the bank?"

"Miss Cooper spelled that out in her will. Her estate paid for one year of training and I was supposed to start when I came to Huntingford General."

"Why didn't you start at the bank?"

She told him about Mr. Charlesworth's secretary sending her to Personnel. "I think Mr. Walker was talking with the hospital's Mr. Holmes when Mr. Walker's assistant brought in my application. Mr. Walker sent me over here and I've been here ever since." Maggie smiled and added, "I think I'm kind of lend-leased to the hospital."

"Do you like working here?"

"Yes, but sometimes I worry that I'm not doing what Miss Cooper wanted me to do. I owe her everything."

"What about your parents?"

"I went to Crosswell when I was ten, and then, when I was twelve, Miss Cooper became my guardian. I've never heard from my parents or my two brothers."

"Did your parents abandon you, or what?"

"I suppose abandon describes it. Mama had ambitions to become a singer and she just left one day. Daddy went to find her. I was supposed to go to somebody's house and stay till he got back, but I stayed at home. Somebody reported to Social Services that I was living alone. That's when Social Services sent Miss Cherney, who brought me to Crosswell. I'm 22 now."

"Where do you live? Does this job pay enough to let you live in a decent neighborhood?"

Maggie sipped her tea again before she answered. Mr. Duncan's caution about revealing her inheritance popped into her mind. "I live in a duplex on Lombard Street. I'm doing just fine."

"So, if you eventually go back to the bank, then what? What are you going to do for ... well ... just fun?"

"I've never told anyone this, not even Miss Cooper. I'd like to find out if I can sing. I think I could play the piano by ear ... I'm thinking of getting a piano ... maybe a used one ... maybe a voice teacher?"

"Then what?"

"If my voice teacher tells me I can sing ..." Maggie stopped in mid-sentence. "I'll sing in church. I don't want to entertain people or wear skimpy clothes like the singers on TV." She glanced at her watch. "I've got to get back to work. Thanks for the tea!"

Dr. Allen pushed his chair under the table also. "How about your afternoon break? By the way, I'm divorced so it's okay for me to take you to tea! How do you get to work?"

"Miss Cooper left me her car."

With that said, Maggie placed her empty cup on a large tray by the cafeteria door and went back to her office and resumed her filing.

Dr. Allen poured himself another cup of coffee and thought about Maggie. It might be fun to take her to a few nightclubs and let her listen to their singers. He wondered what she would wear and decided to ask her to go with him the next time he went by Medical Records.

Chapter 9

On Saturday, Maggie went to Parker's to find a dress to wear to the nightclub with Dr. Allen. The sizes 8s on the rack were too short, barely covering her knees, but the 10s were too big. She finally chose an emerald green wool knit with a full skirt and long sleeves. The bodice gathered gently from the neckline, ending in a cummerbund effect. She added black flats and put on a short pearl necklace.

She could almost hear Miss Cooper.

Clothes should fit the body properly, Margaret, not as if the body were poured into them; neither should they droop like a bed sheet.

Maggie thought of her again when she applied the pink lipstick and used a little on her cheeks, blending it in with her fingertips. She wiped off most of it. She scorned eye makeup. Miss Cooper had not approved of it, describing it as trashy. Last, she placed a hand towel around her neck then brushed her hair, which fell past her shoulders.

Dr. Allen called for her at eight. When she greeted him in her usual manner, he said, "My name is Richard. I wish you would call me that."

Call a doctor by his given name? The thought surprised Maggie. After a moment, she decided Miss Cooper would approve when they were away from work, so she agreed.

Richard held Maggie's arm as they walked into the Lion's Lair. They sat at a small table and he ordered scotch and soda for himself. Maggie had ginger ale, which he called a Shirley Temple.

He watched her as the singer started her rendition of 'Moon River'. The singer's costume left little to the imagination. Her voice was low and 'throaty'. She sang a few more songs that Maggie didn't recognize.

Maggie glanced away from time to time, and Richard guessed the singer's scanty dress embarrassed her.

"Well, what do you think," Richard asked on the way home.

"I could never appear in public dressed like that … especially with so many people watching."

When they reached the duplex, Richard held her hand as they said goodnight.

Dr. Richard Allen spent the rest of the evening thinking about Maggie, the file clerk who could be so much more. He couldn't get her out of his mind.

Chapter 10

Maggie, feeling guilty about not working at the bank, called Mr. Dawson one Monday when she came into work at the hospital.

The attorney answered the phone with a crisp, 'Dawson'.

"Good morning, Mr. Dawson, this is Margaret Monahan … from Crosswell," she added in case he had forgotten.

"Nice to hear from you, Miss Monahan. How are things going at the bank?"

"That's why I called. I've been on loan to Huntingford General. I've just finished updating their files in Medical Records."

"I see. How did it happen you're over there instead of the bank?"

"Oh, well, I couldn't get in to see Mr. Charlesworth and his secretary sent me to Personnel. They needed someone at the hospital, so the Personnel Director sent me over here to help out, but I really want to learn about banking. Miss Cooper paid for my training and I feel I owe it to her to try."

"Of course, you do. How are things going at the duplex?"

"Mr. Scott is very nice and keeps up the yard work. He's very particular about the windows and sometimes he points out interesting things about the flowerbeds. Could you contact Mr. Charlesworth again? I think I'll stay home a week before starting at the bank."

"Certainly I will contact him. You'll hear from him sometime this week. He'll contact you at Medical Records. Would mornings or afternoons be more convenient for you to visit with Mr. Charlesworth?"

"Mornings would be fine. Thank you, Mr. Dawson."

Maggie dusted her desk again and stood looking at the completed files.

***

Anthony Dawson lost no time contacting Curtis Charlesworth, President of the Magnolia Trust and Savings. Charlesworth was in a meeting and his secretary assured Dawson that she would get the message to him as soon as he returned to his office.

Charlesworth frowned as he read the phone message his secretary, Grace Bovenkamp, had placed on his desk. The memo read: 'Mr. Anthony Dawson called about the employment of a Miss Margaret Monahan from Crosswell. Please call him at your earliest convenience. He left word with his office to page him when you call."

Charlesworth buzzed on the intercom for Grace. "What about Miss Monahan? How is she working out? What department is she in? Get Dawson. Something must be wrong or he wouldn't have called me. He never calls me … always talks to other people in the bank."

"Hello, Anthony, this is Curtis Charlesworth."

Dawson's voice, when he answered, held just a hint of the frustration he felt.

"Look Curtis, as you are aware, Rachel

Cooper's will left money in her estate to pay for the training of one of the Crosswell girls, her ward, Margaret Monahan. Some pencil pusher at your place loaned her to Huntingford General to update files. Curtis, did you know she has a degree in Elementary Education and a minor in Accounting? To say nothing of the fact that she takes shorthand and types well enough to be anybody's administrative assistant. I don't think you would want Miss Monahan to become unhappy with the bank and draw out her assets, which, as you know, are considerable."

He continued before Charlesworth could speak.

"You need to personally take her to the department where she will start her training and introduce her to the staff. No filing. I think she ought to start as a teller. She'll get the feel for the bank and associate with people who will help her. No one is to know the arrangements of Miss Cooper's will. I hope it won't be necessary for me to counsel her to draw out her assets from this bank."

Dawson turned his voice from firm to friendly. "How's the family?"

Charlesworth answered Dawson with a hearty, 'just fine', hung up and barked an order. "Grace, get me a copy of Miss Monahan's portfolio. We probably have a copy of Cooper's will, and Dawson has already sent us a check for her training. Call the hospital, Medical Records. I'll talk to Miss Monahan myself. Good God, loaning her out to the hospital as a file clerk! Any attorney but Dawson would have closed out her account and sued the bank for fraud. Thank God, he's on our Board of Directors!"

Maggie was watering one of Bertha's plants when the phone rang.

"Miss Monahan, this is Curtis Charlesworth with Magnolia Trust and Savings. I'm terribly sorry about the mix up. When would it be convenient for you to start your training?"

"I plan to stay home the rest of this week. I can come in next Monday, if that's convenient."

"Fine, would ten o'clock be all right with you?"

"Yes, thank you."

"Please come directly to my office. I'll be waiting for you. I think we'll start you as a teller. No filing."

"I don't mind filing. I take dictation, also."

"No filing," he repeated. "After you learn the teller's job, we'll move you into investment banking. You can use your secretarial skills there to help you learn. Our Mr. Barnes is in charge of that department."

"Thank you, Mr. Charlesworth. I'll be there at ten on Monday morning."

***

Charlesworth, true to his word, personally escorted Maggie to Alice Fogarty's office. The sign on the door read, 'Alice Fogarty, Supervisor of Tellers'.

He opened the door without knocking. "Alice, this is Miss Margaret Monahan. She starts work today as a trainee in your department."

Alice greeted Maggie with a smile. "I'm happy to know you, Miss Monahan. Shall we call you that?"

"Please call me Maggie."

Charlesworth hesitated at the door. "By the way, Miss Monahan wants to learn the banking business. She has a degree in Elementary Education and a Minor in Accounting. She also takes shorthand, but she is not to do any secretarial work. Only teach her how to be the best teller she can be. When she's ready to move on to other departments of the bank, please notify me personally. You need not go through Personnel."

"Yes, sir." Alice turned to Maggie. "Maggie, I'm glad to have you with us. Some of the tellers are on their coffee break. Let's go meet them."

On the way to the employees' lounge, Maggie asked Alice what she should wear.

"What you have on now is just fine. We've trained Crosswell girls before and they come to us knowing pretty much what to wear. I've read about Miss Cooper. She came into the bank about once a month. Mr. Charlesworth filled me in about her will. I don't think it is necessary for you to explain to your co-workers that you're a graduate of Crosswell or the university, for that matter. I see you live on Lombard. Just tell the others, if they should ask, that you live on Lombard in a duplex. They'll assume you're renting and that's okay. I'm sure you'll enjoy your work at the bank."

Several of the tellers looked toward the door as Maggie and Alice came into the room.

"Good morning, girls, this is Maggie Monahan, a trainee. She will need all of us to help her. She is going to learn all about banking and is starting in our department."

Alice helped herself to coffee and showed Maggie where to find the tea bags. A carafe held hot water.

Fifteen minutes late, everyone left the lounge. Maggie was assigned to work with Norma Peters.

Maggie smiled at the customer who slid her deposit across the counter. She had begun her training.

At five o'clock, Maggie was glad to get off her feet. When she reached home, the first thing she did was kick off her shoes. Almost without thinking, she picked them up and placed them neatly in her bedroom closet.

Miss Cooper never kicked off her shoes … ever.

Chapter 11

Maggie had been at the bank for about six months.

One Saturday morning, she walked from her duplex to the park about five blocks away. The day was overcast, but rain had not been predicted. She tried to concentrate on the journal she brought from home, but found it difficult.

Some children played with a large ball near the bench where she sat. The kids were having a great time playing three-corner catch. The oldest, a girl, appeared to be about ten, a boy about seven, and a smaller boy about four. The girl's hair hung past her shoulders in auburn waves. Her jeans were two sizes too big and she'd rolled the shirt sleeves past her elbows. Maggie decided the girl was too thin. The boys' jeans showed signs of many washings. The kids looked clean, though.

It began to rain about half an hour after she started reading the journal. The rain began with drops at first then steadier, then almost a downpour. She heard a snatch of conversation as she hurried out of the park.

"We can't go to the shelter house; it's not open yet. We got to go home. Mom said to come home if it rained."

Maggie arrived home ahead of the downpour and backed her car out of the garage. She drove to the park, hoping to catch the kids and take them home before they got too wet. She caught up with them about three blocks from the park. A fall wind came up and blew the girl's hair over her face. The four-year old clung to her hand, trying to keep up with her.

Maggie slowed her car and rolled down the window. "Hello, may I give you a lift? I left the park when it started to rain. I live on Lombard and work at the bank. I'd be happy to give you a lift home."

The girl hesitated only a moment. Mama had warned her about getting into cars, but this was a lady and the three of them were together.

"Okay," the girl answered, and herded the boys into the back seat of the car, then slammed the door shut.

"Now," Maggie said, "what is your address?"

"1210 Fortune Street. We live in the back."

The address was a dilapidated apartment building needing paint. There were toys strewn about the front yard, which boasted a small patch of grass. The screen door was torn and the front window boarded up. Around back, garbage cans were scattered in what at one time was probably a yard. An old tire holding sand sat forlornly under a scrawny tree. The kids jumped out of the car and disappeared through the single door.

Maggie wondered who the children were and what happened to bring them to such a place to live. She speculated on her way home. Probably a father who had left and a mother who struggled to make ends meet. She probably worked a dead-end job and left the girl to take care of the younger ones.

'I was ten when I arrived at Crosswell', came

60

unbidden to her mind. Maggie hadn't thought of her home before she went to Crosswell in a long time, but the sight of the rundown apartment building brought it all back into sharp focus. She remembered the hungry nights and the impossible clothes her mother bought at garage sales.

When Maggie walked into her duplex, the first thing she did after setting her umbrella in the foyer, was to look up the address in the City Directory. It listed four tenants, two on the main floor, front and rear, and two on the second floor, front and rear. The first floor rear apartment listed four names: Julie, Jennifer 10, Jason 6, and Jordan 4. The last name was Webb. Julie, the mother, worked at the Boulevard Café, as a waitress.

Maggie changed her clothes to a pair of gray slacks with a gray tailored shirt. She drove to the Boulevard Café, across town from Lombard, and slid into a booth. She pulled the menu from behind the napkin holder and studied it.

The special was stuffed peppers, which she didn't like, so she ordered a hot beef sandwich. It would be her main meal, so she ordered a salad also. She wouldn't have to cook any supper.

The waitress who poured cups of coffee stopped at Maggie's table. The name 'Julie' was machine embroidered on the front pocket.

"Hello, Julie, I'm Maggie Monahan. I gave your children a lift home from the park. It was raining hard and the wind had come up. The shelter house wasn't open and the children would have been soaked."

Julie smiled. "Thanks, I appreciate that. The kids go to the park on Saturdays. Jennifer's pretty good to watch Jason and Jordan."

Julie paused a minute longer and Maggie said, "I was happy to give them a lift. Perhaps I'll see them again before winter. I like to go to the park on Saturdays."

"Thanks again," Julie said, and turned to pour a second cup of decaf for the man in the booth across from Maggie's table.

Maggie picked up a few things in the grocery store when she left the café and thought about her new acquaintances on her way home.

***

Maggie couldn't remember when the idea first formed to get Julie and her children out of that rundown apartment. As she cleared away the few dishes from supper, rinsed them, and put them in the dishwasher, she made a mental note to look for houses for sale in the Sunday paper.

She would ask Mr. Scott to go with her to find a house ... no, she would not ask him. She could not discuss finances with Mr. Scott, and it was then she decided that she would ask Dr. Allen for advice. A sixth sense told her that neither Attorney Anthony Dawson nor Mr. Charlesworth at the bank would approve.

On her 'things to do' list for Monday, she made a note to call Dr. Allen during her break at the bank. She would ask him to stop by any evening convenient for him. She hoped he would come.

Chapter 12

On her Friday morning break at the bank, Maggie went to the outside lobby and used one of the pay phones to call Dr. Allen. He answered in only two rings.

"Richard Allen, Pathology."

"Hello, Dr. Allen. This is Maggie Monahan." She rushed on before she could lose her nerve. "I know it's asking a lot, but could you stop over at my place after work? There's something I want to discuss with you."

"Sure." He hesitated a second then asked, "Are you okay, Maggie?"

"Oh, yes, I'm okay. I just want to talk to you about something I want to do."

"What time will you be home?"

"About five."

"I can be there by five-thirty. Tell me your address again."

"935 West Lombard, the green duplex. Thank you, Richard. I'll see you at five-thirty."

***

Richard Allen had turned 33 the day before he called on Maggie in response to her phone call. Six feet, sandy hair, blue eyes, and a sense of contentment after his divorce. There had been no children.

Maggie answered the door promptly.

"Hi, Maggie. You're looking great!"

"Thank you, so are you. Please come in." She led the way into her living room and motioned him to a chair.

He settled his long frame then asked, "Now what's this all about, Maggie? I got scared when you first called."

"I apologize! That didn't occur to me." She plunged right in with her request. "I want to get a mother and her three children out of a dump, an apartment, if you can call it that, but I don't know how to do it. I don't want the bank to know, and I'm afraid to ask Mr. Scott or Mr. Charlesworth, and Mr. Dawson would never approve of me spending the money."

Surprise showed on his face, but he answered calmly enough. "Tell me about this woman and her kids."

"Well, Dr. Allen, I …"

"Maggie, you agreed to call me Richard, remember? We're not in the hospital now, and I'm really pleased you called me, and that you trust me to help you. So, Richard, huh?"

"All right, Richard. I met this woman, really her children, in the park recently. I can't get them out of my mind. The girl is about ten. The same age I was when I went to Crosswell. There are two little boys, Jason about six and Jordan about four. I looked up the family in the City Directory, then I went to the restaurant where the mother, Julie, works. She's much thinner than Mama was when I came to Crosswell."

Maggie took a deep breath, then her words tumbled out faster. "Oh, Richard, the place is terrible. The apartment is so small, just the back of a remodeled place they call an apartment building. I wonder where

64

they all sleep. I wonder if they each have a bed. Miss Cooper left me this place and I have so much to be thankful for, and Julie's struggling to make it. What can I do, Richard? Can I buy a house and let them live in it? Will you help me find one near the school? They go to Jefferson Elementary now, and I don't believe she would want to move them to another school. I hated changing schools. You never make friends, and I don't believe you learn as much as you should."

To her utter amazement, Maggie began to cry.

Richard came over and put his arm around her. "Hey, it's going to be all right." He pulled out a large white handkerchief and handed it to her. "Now, Maggie, let's talk this through."

"I understand that Miss Cooper left you her home and her car. You told me that, but you didn't mention money. Houses are expensive!"

Maggie hesitated a long moment, remembering Mr. Dawson's words about keeping her financial matters quiet. She decided to tell Richard at least part of the story. "She left me an investment that will allow me to do this. I earn more than enough to support myself, so I won't be destitute."

He studied her face, then spoke hesitantly. "I know you've had the breaks, and you want to pass on what Miss Cooper did for you. However, here you have a family, not just one little girl who showed up on your doorstep. I think you can help them, yes, but help Julie in a way she can also help herself. Don't just hand it to her. Let her work for it the same as she's working for her rent now. She needs to feel she is making it on her own, but it's okay to give her a helping hand."

Maggie nodded slowly. "Yes, that's better, but how do I go about it?"

"Now that I think about it, Maggie, there's a guy in accounting at the hospital who inherited an older home in the Jefferson area from an aunt. He wants to sell on contract. I don't know why he doesn't want to go through a realtor or his bank. I think he would consider a thousand down and monthly payments. If you think you need to subsidize payments, well, you could do that."

"I can afford the down payment and to subsidize payments, too, if necessary."

"Would you like to go look at it tomorrow? Let's see, tomorrow's Saturday and he works in the morning at the hospital. I'll stop by and pick up the key. In the meantime, why don't you get into your jeans and we'll go have a bite to eat on River Road and drive by the place."

"I don't have any jeans, but I do have slacks. Will that be okay?"

"Sure, you look great in anything."

Maggie went to the bedroom and put on a pair of black slacks with a belt. She slipped into a knit top and put on a multi-colored shell necklace, which had been among Miss Cooper's things. Maggie was so happy that Richard could help her with the house project that she forgot to be critical of herself, weighing her attire on the standards Miss Cooper had laid down for the girls at Crosswell. Had she taken time to do that, Maggie would have removed the knit top, as it outlined her breasts and accentuated her small waist. Miss Cooper would have had her take it off, saying ladies should always wear blouses. Maggie had taken down her hair from the bun that she always wore for work. It hung in waves to her shoulders.

"I'm ready, shall we go?"

Richard held open the door for her. She waited till he stepped outside and then she locked the door.

The restaurant was about 20 minutes away, an Italian place with large red-checkered tablecloths and huge red napkins at each place setting. Richard held out her chair for her, saying, "I didn't have much lunch today, so I'm starved. I'm going to have the spaghetti special with salad. How about you, Maggie?"

"The spaghetti will be fine for me, also. I can't remember if we ever had it at Crosswell. Perhaps Miss Cooper didn't care for it."

"How about some wine," Richard asked. "A small glass won't hurt you … actually it will relax you."

She hesitated, not wanting to refuse but felt she must.

"Richard. Miss Cooper …"

He shook his head, a rueful smile on his face. "Maggie, try not to think about what Miss Cooper would want every time you do something. You've got to decide what it is you want to do … she's not here anymore … a small glass, okay."

Maggie smiled. "Well, all right, but just one."

For the rest of the meal, Maggie tried very hard

not to think of Miss Cooper. Once she started to mention her, and found Richard smiling.

When the waiter brought the check, Maggie, without thinking, took a ten dollar bill from her purse and laid it on the table.

Richard put his hand over hers. "Maggie, please, my treat."

Maggie wondered if Miss Cooper would expect her to pay for her own food, but, then, resolutely put that lady out of her mind. Richard was right. She had to stand on her own two feet now.

As they drove toward his friend's house, Richard told her about the neighborhood. "The house is about four blocks from the school and the kids won't need to take the bus. It's on Vine Street in the 600 block." They drove on a few minutes, and turned onto Vine and drove to the middle of the block. The house number read 626.

The house was a one-and-a-half story wood frame building with faded paint. The front yard was average size for the neighborhood, and the grass had been recently cut. A wide porch flanked the front door.

Maggie and Richard got out of the car and walked around the house together. He judged there to be a living room, dining room and kitchen with two bedrooms on the main floor and a large room upstairs with slanted ceiling. They couldn't tell if the house had a full basement, but the backyard went to the alley. A small bank of bushes stood at the rear of the house and some evergreens stood by the front steps to the house. That was the extent of the landscaping.

"This place needs painting badly," Richard said. "You can get someone to spray paint it, and Julie could paint the trim on the windows and the porch as well as the outside doors. The landlord usually buys the paint."

"Yes, it certainly does need paint. Shall I offer her a month's rent to paint? What about the inside?"

"Whoa, Maggie! You haven't bought the place yet. Let's wait and see what it looks like inside. Then you will know what kind of deal you can offer Julie."

With that, they walked to the car and Richard took Maggie home.

"Good night, Maggie. I'll be around after work for you. We'll look at the house and see what kind of deal we can make with the owner."

Maggie waved goodbye as Richard turned on the ignition. He waved back and drove slowly to his condo.

Chapter 13

Richard threw his keys on the table by the front door of his condo on Piedmont Boulevard. He walked to the kitchen, poured himself a glass of orange juice and leaned against the counter.

He thought about Maggie Monahan when she worked at the hospital, wearing formal business clothes every day, her fingers speeding over the typewriter keys. Her self-assurance as far as her skills were concerned, but total reliance on the proverbs of Miss Cooper to guide her through everyday situations.

He thought he ought to help her get over being so dependent on the ghost of Miss Cooper, and he'd begin with telling her to buy some jeans, a corduroy jacket, and a turtleneck top. He'd take her to the Riverfront outdoor concert tomorrow night. He called her.

"Maggie, after we look at the house and have lunch, maybe over at the restaurant where Julie works, we could take in the Riverfront concert. It's very informal. I'll bring along a blanket for us to sit on. Why don't you go shopping after lunch and get some jeans and a jacket and stuff?"

"Miss Cooper said … I'm sorry, Richard. I'm really trying not to preface every sentence with her name."

"That's okay, Maggie, nobody changes over night. Now tell me, what did Miss Cooper say about jeans?"

"She said pants were the province of men.

Ladies always wear skirts and blouses ... no knit tops because they might appear to be ..." she paused ever so slightly, "... suggestive. She did allow what she called 'dress pants' on rare occasion."

"This is the seventies, Maggie. Everybody else at the concert, even old ladies, will be in jeans. Tell you what, why don't we go over to Parker's Department Store to the women's shop on the second floor. I'll wait for you in the waiting room where all the guys sit while their wives spend their money." He quickly added, "Lots of single folks shop there, too. Did the bank issue you a credit card?"

"Of course, but I've never used it." Miss Cooper was adamant about being in debt, but Maggie wouldn't tell him that.

"Good, break it in. I'll be by at eleven o'clock tomorrow and we'll go look at the house.

***

Maggie put on a skirt and blouse and brushed her hair, letting it hang loose. She didn't bother with make-up—she only owned a pale pink lipstick.

Richard arrived promptly at eleven and they drove to the house on Vine Street. Nearing the front door, Richard took the key from his pocket and handed it to Maggie. She hurried ahead of him, then unlocked the door, and held it open for him.

The owners had left on the utilities, and Maggie flipped the switch in the small vestibule.

The wallpaper had long ago faded and the dark woodwork showed a fine layer of dust. They stepped into a narrow hall. On the left, an arch separated the living room and dining room, and the kitchen lay beyond. Two small rooms were on the other side of the hall. They climbed the stairs leaving handprints on the dusty railing. The bathroom was upstairs, and three small rooms were under the slanted ceiling. A small stairway led to an attic. They walked downstairs and started a more detailed tour of the house.

The living room wallpaper was faded also. At one time, the pattern was small flowers. The hardwood floor was badly in need of refinishing. The dining room had wallpaper with large flowers. It, too, was so faded it was hard to make out the original design. The kitchen appliances appeared to be original to the house. Inexpensive cabinets, at one time painted white, were on one wall only. The door to one cabinet hung crookedly. The lower cabinets were under the sink, and a cabinet with a linoleum cover had four drawers. The remaining walls were bare. There was no refrigerator.

Richard lit one of the burners on an ancient gas stove. "It works okay. I'll bet you couldn't wreck that heavy stove with a tank."

A back porch protected the kitchen from the winter winds. Wide boards covered the floor; the paint was long gone.

As they walked back through the kitchen, Maggie paused by the sink. "Look, Richard, there's a window over the sink. I always wanted a kitchen with a window when I was a little girl."

"What else did you want when you were a little girl, Maggie?"

She hesitated. This was something she preferred not to remember. "Sometimes we were hungry. Mama would just take off at times and leave us. Then Daddy would go looking for her."

Her voice trembled and Richard quickly changed the subject.

"Let's go upstairs and see what the plumbing is like. Looks like the lady never did anything to this house in at least fifty years. No wonder Dan wants to get rid of it."

The carpet on the stairs looked fifty years old, Maggie thought. It would have to come up.

The bathroom was larger than standard-sized bathrooms in newer homes. The floor tiles were tiny hexagons. The walls had been robin's egg blue at one time, and the bathtub had a huge rust stain from the faucet to the drain. The washbasin was cracked and one faucet was gone. An ancient medicine cabinet with a speckled mirror hung over the washbowl. The toilet stool would also need to be replaced.

Richard turned on the water in the tub. The pressure was fine.

There were two medium sized bedrooms and one smaller room, which could be a third bedroom, but had been used for storage. Two broken chairs, an old dresser, and boxes of odds and ends, were in the middle of the floor, and against one wall were springs with a very worn mattress standing beside it.

Maggie broke the silence.

"Do you think this room can ever be fixed up for a little girl, Richard?"

"Sure. You'd be surprised what a little fresh paint will do for a room. New curtains, I suppose, and just a few pieces of basic furniture ... a bed ... dresser and stuff ... and, of course, this mattress has to go. We could use this dresser, if it's painted." Richard ran his hand over the top of the dresser and looked closer at the drawers. No, couldn't paint this. The dresser and headboard looked like walnut.

They stood in silence for a moment, then Richard swallowed a sigh and spoke. "You still want to fix up this place for Julie, don't you?"

"Oh, yes, Richard." Her eyes were shining. She didn't know where she would get the money ... Mr. Dawson controlled her trust fund ... but she would manage some way.

"Okay. The next thing we must do is call an inspector and determine how sound the building is. It wouldn't do to buy it without being sure it wasn't going to fall down from termite damage, or some such."

"Oh." Maggie looked worried. "I hadn't thought about that. How long will it take?"

"I'll make a phone call. My former brother-in-law does this sort of thing for a living. We get along fine, in spite of his sister's divorce." He punched in a number. "Hi, Chuck, Richard here. How's your schedule? I need your expertise as quickly as I can get it."

Maggie listened to the one-sided conversation.

"That's great, Chuck! I owe you." Richard clicked his cell phone shut. "He's coming over now."

74

"Wonderful!" Relief poured over Maggie like a soft rain. Everything was working out perfectly.

Richard smiled at her. "Now, while we wait what do you think of this? You buy the materials and let her do most of the work, painting and stuff, and give her a break on the rent each month until the painting's done." He tapped his forehead. "But, wait, Maggie, I'm getting ahead of myself. We don't know how much Dan wants for the house, or whether Julie will even like it. Don't you think we'd better find out these little items first?"

"Yes, I suppose we should, but Richard, couldn't we do something to the inside before she sees it? It's so dismal. I wouldn't like it. I wouldn't want to live here the way it is now! Can we fix it?"

"We?"

"Oh, Richard, I'm sorry. All I want you to do is advise me. You don't have to do any of the work. I don't know any paint contractors or people who take off wallpaper or refinish floors."

"Whoa, Maggie! I was teasing. I wouldn't miss this for the world, but let's take this one step at a time. Let's think about the pluses and minuses of the property." He turned toward the door. "Here's Chuck, now, so we can eliminate the most important plus or minus question immediately."

Maggie followed them around, watching anxiously as Chuck tapped walls and inspected the roof. She didn't follow them under the house, though, but waited anxiously outside the crawl space until they emerged, dust covered, but with a reassuring nod.

Half an hour later, Chuck pronounced the house sound. He waved Richard off when the latter asked what he owed. "I'll call you the next time I have an ache or pain!"

Maggie and Richard watched him drive away.

"Okay, now where were we?" he asked. "Ah, yes, you can hire it all done and give it to her. From a purely business standpoint, you'd have to charge her quite a bit for rent to recoup your investment."

"I can't get it out of my mind that I have a decent place to live and I didn't work for any of it!"

"In a sense you did, Maggie. Didn't you have responsibilities at Crosswell? Didn't you clean and dust and that sort of thing?"

"Well, of course, I did. All of the girls had chores, but I don't think of that as paying for living there."

"Nevertheless, that's what it was."

Maggie could be stubborn when she chose. "I still feel like I didn't work to have what I do."

"Julie is not you, Maggie. She's had a husband and now is supporting her three kids. I think you should let her earn part of the cost of repair for the privilege of living in this house, and giving her ownership in the project. That's what dignity is all about, Maggie."

She gave in. "Okay, can we go see what the owner wants for it?"

"Righto. Let me do the talking. It's going to cost you some bucks to make this place fit to live in, and that ought to keep the price down. If we can get a good

76

deal, you can afford to fix it up."

"If Julie doesn't want it, could I fix it up for another poor family?"

Richard shook his head at her albeit with a smile on his face. "Maggie, Maggie, she'll want it, especially if you give her an option to buy it. Let's go."

He locked the door and drove to Dan Birchard's house to close the deal.

Chapter 14

Dan Birchard stood at the door when they arrived and held it open for Maggie and Richard to come in.

"Hi, guys. Maggie, I remember you from the hospital. I'm in accounting. We had quite a mix up on getting you paid, but we finally did. Sit down. Can I offer you something to drink?"

When they declined, he said, "Now about the house. It's old, old, old. Aunt Lavina never had the health or the money to fix it up, but it could be livable. I imagine you've had an inspector look at it?"

Richard answered in the affirmative. "It's sound."

Dan turned toward Maggie. "Are you figuring on living there someday?"

"No," Richard answered quickly. "Maggie has her own place, and you know I have my own condo. We're going to buy it together and fix it up for a rental property. We have a family in mind. Has three kids."

"Okay, how does $10,000 sound to you? A thousand down and payments of $100 a month. As is. I'll sell it to you on contract. I won't have capital gains tax, and no realtor and no bank. I have a standard contract you can sign, and we'll get Bertha Gallaway in Records to witness it. How soon can you sign?"

"Slow down, Dan!" Richard held up his hand cop-fashion. "Maggie, what do you think about the price and the payments?"

Maggie hardly knew what to think. Richard's

comment that they would purchase the house together surprised, yet after a moment, pleased her. She could manage her half without applying to Mr. Dawson to invade the trust account. She nodded to Richard.

"Yes, I can manage my share."

Richard turned back to Dan. "So can I, so it's a deal. Maggie, my schedule is more flexible than yours is. When do you want to sign the contract?"

"Monday," she said quickly after pulling a daily planner out of her purse. "I have to be at the bank by eight, so could we make it right after work? I could get off a little early and be at the hospital at five."

The trio visited awhile about what was going on at Huntington General and then Maggie and Richard left for Parker's Department Store.

They took the elevator to the second floor where Richard flopped into a chair by a table containing several magazines. He took one from the top and slowly turned the pages.

Maggie went straight to the sales person and asked for help. Miss Cooper had never gone through the racks of clothing; instead, she always told the sales person what she needed and the price range.

Maggie pointed to the rack of blazers. "I need one in beige … a size 8, some jeans and a brown turtleneck."

The sales person quickly found her size, went to where the jeans were hanging and found a 24-inch waist, then the turtleneck. She expertly tossed the clothing over her arm and motioned for Maggie to follow her to the fitting room.

Maggie felt strangely uneasy when she had on the entire outfit. The jeans fit just right and the turtleneck went well with the blazer. Maggie suppressed a desire to tell the sales person to get a skirt. Instead, she went to the small waiting room where Richard was reading. He was the only one there.

He gave a low whistle. "You look great, Maggie. You're a woman of the seventies. Give her your credit card and we're all set. She'll box up the duds you wore here."

The bill came close to a hundred dollars and, for a fleeting moment, Maggie wondered if Miss Cooper would approve. Not the jeans, of course, but Miss Cooper had always stressed quality. These purchases met that requirement, so Maggie decided her old mentor would approve of that anyway.

The credit card from Magnolia Trust read: Margaret Monahan, the next line a series of numbers, and the VISA logo. Maggie gave the card to the saleslady and took the receipt and the box of the clothing she'd worn into the store. Then she and Richard left the store.

From there, Richard drove to the restaurant where Julie worked. Julie waved to them as they came in.

"Hello, Julie," Maggie said. "We're going to eat lunch here. Could you come over and sit with us during your break?"

Julie set glasses of water at each place. "Sure can. I get my break at one and it's twelve now. What will you have?"

Richard smiled and said, "Let's have spaghetti again. It's great and I'm starved."

"I'll have the same," Maggie told her. "And some hot tea, please, no cream or sugar."

"Coffee for me," Richard added.

When Julie stepped away, Maggie spoke in a low tone to Richard. "Do you really like the house?"

"Yes. It's okay for people to start out, and I think Julie will appreciate the chance to live in a house."

"I thought you must like it a lot since you said you would join me in buying it." She eyed him closely. "You surprised me, by the way. I wasn't expecting it."

"Well, to tell the truth, I wasn't expecting it either! The words just popped out of my mouth and in that instant I knew it was the right thing to do."

"Shall we tell her right away about the rent and credit for fixing it up? Shall we give Dan the down payment in cash?"

"No," he replied. "I don't think cash is a good idea. We need to have a record. For Julie's sake and ours, we need to keep this transaction on a business basis. We can get some checks printed temporarily for, let's see, how about M and R Investments?"

"That sounds good, but shouldn't it be R and M instead?"

"No, this is alphabetical. That's the best way since we're equal partners. We can use my post office box number. Dan indicated he would leave the utilities on for a week or so until we get them changed over."

"Oh, Richard, you should be the senior partner

... I would never have thought of all this!"

"I'm happy with being equal partners," he assured her. "Let's find out how much Julie is paying for rent, and, if she can manage the house rental and utilities. Then we'll go from there."

"Will she have to pay a deposit?"

"Probably, but we can give her a hand with that. Whatever the deposits are, for lights, gas, and water, we could split down the middle and pay ourselves back from the rent. How does that sound to you?"

Maggie touched his hand. "Richard, I'm so glad you know all this, because I don't! Mr. Dawson did all that for the duplex. All I did was move in."

Julie returned with tea and coffee.

They waited again until she disappeared into the kitchen.

"Couldn't I just fix up the kitchen a little bit, Richard? It's so dreary! Do you think lemon yellow would be okay?"

"I think it would be fine, but don't you think Julie might not care for yellow? We talked about Julie needing to have ownership in refurbishing the house. She needs to develop confidence in herself ... that she can manage a house."

Maggie sipped her tea in silence for a moment. "Do you think I'm self-confident, Richard?"

"In your professional life, yes, you are, but not in your personal life. You always have the ghost of Miss Cooper interfering with any decisions you make." He spoke gently.

"She's the only person who ever cared about

me." Maggie's voice was so soft Richard had to strain to hear.

"I know."

"She left me this letter. She said someday I might choose to marry and have a family and that's okay ... but I have no idea whom I would marry. I'm certainly not like those women you see in movies and on TV. I'm not like anyone at the bank or at the hospital either."

"You're gaining in self-confidence every day, so when the time comes to marry, you'll know, Maggie. You'll know. And I'd bet anything you'll feel Miss Cooper is giving you her blessing."

They ate the spaghetti that Julie brought and talked of other things until Julie slid into the booth beside Maggie promptly at one o'clock.

And just as promptly, Maggie began talking. "Richard and I have bought a house for investment and we want to fix it up as rental property. Would you be interested, Julie?"

Without waiting for an answer, Maggie rushed on describing the house. "And it's only four blocks from Jefferson School."

Richard cut in with the business end of the discussion. "We want to give our new tenant three months' rent for fixing up the inside, painting and things like that. We'll supply the paint. We'll also hire someone to paint the outside, which is a much bigger job."

Julie didn't hesitate. "I'd love a house, but I'm not sure I could afford the rent and utilities, stuff like that."

Richard questioned her about her finances. "How much are you paying for rent in your apartment?"

"A hundred and fifty for rent, and I pay my lights, gas and telephone."

Richard pulled out his pocket planner. "I think that would work with the house. One fifty a month for rent plus utilities; the investment company will pay the deposits."

Julie bit her lip. "Are you going to sell it then, when it's fixed up?"

"No," Richard replied. "Remember I said we bought it for investment property. We're going to rent it to get our money back. If we buy another house and fix it up, and decide to sell this one, we'll offer it to you first, if you're interested. So, here's the deal, Julie: One hundred fifty dollars a month plus the utilities. We will pay the deposits. The first three months are rent-free in exchange for work … painting, etc. We take possession Monday evening at five o'clock, and we'll meet you here at the restaurant at five-thirty. We'll take you to see the house and go from there."

Julie's eyes filled with tears. "Why are you helping me?"

Before Maggie could answer, Richard said quietly, "We're passing on a blessing which we received from someone else."

To ease the emotional moment, Maggie asked, "Julie, do you like lemon yellow?"

Julie could hardly get the word out. "I love

lemon yellow. It lets in the sunshine even on rainy days." She was too overcome with their generosity to wonder about the color question. Julie held both hands toward them. Richard and Maggie each squeezed one, then left the restaurant.

They drove to the waterfront and sat on a blanket he had brought. Richard put his arm around Maggie. Her eyes were bright with anticipation of enjoying the music.

On the way home, Maggie told Richard twice how much she enjoyed the music. She went into her duplex, and Richard stood at the door until he saw her lights go on, then he drove home.

Chapter 15

Maggie arrived at the new house to fix up the kitchen on Tuesday around five o'clock after working at the bank. She brought a metal ladder from her duplex and stopped at the grocery store to buy cleaning supplies. She thought she would work for a couple of hours. Julie had been enthusiastic the evening before when she and Richard brought her to see it.

At ten minutes to seven, she had finished washing the woodwork. She began to feel sick at her stomach. She sat on the bottom step of the ladder and tried to remember what she had eaten. A small roast beef sandwich and a green salad ... no snacks. She brushed her hand across her face, which felt warm. A sharp pain in her lower right abdomen doubled her over. She stumbled to the bathroom and threw up her lunch. All she wanted to do was to lie down.

Fortunately, Dan had left on the phone service. Maggie called Richard, who answered immediately.

"Richard, could you come over to the house and get me? I feel sick. I have a sharp pain in my side that won't go away. I want to go home." She gasped as another pain struck her.

"Where's the pain, Maggie?"

"In the lower right abdomen, way down."

"Are you vomiting?"

"Yes, I threw up my lunch."

"Can you tell if you have a fever?

"My face feels hot."

"Maggie, just lie on the floor. You may have acute appendicitis."

She put the phone on the bottom step of the ladder and lay down.

When Richard came, he felt her face and gathered her into his arms. "You have to go to the hospital, Maggie. I can get you there quicker than getting an ambulance to come here. Just put your arms around my neck while I lift you." He carried her to the car and placed her gently on the back seat.

They arrived at the hospital in ten minutes, after Richard broke every speed limit getting there. He talked to the emergency room physician, Dr. Foster.

"She's showing the symptoms of acute appendicitis," he said.

Dr. Foster placed a thermometer under Maggie's tongue, and called for a technician to get a blood sample. In a few minutes, the lab reported that Maggie's white cell count was above 10,000.

Dr. Foster turned to Richard. "We'll have to operate. Who's her family doctor?"

Richard replied, "Get Dr. Edwards. He's a topnotch surgeon. Okay, Maggie?"

She smiled weakly. "I don't have a regular doctor. I haven't been sick since I left Crosswell. So, get the surgeon Richard recommended."

Richard nodded and asked, "Can you sign the consent form, Maggie?"

The nurse held the clipboard steady and Maggie scribbled her name. Miss Cooper definitely would not approve of that penmanship, Maggie thought, but couldn't do any better.

Dr. Edwards was making his rounds and came to the ER almost immediately. After reading Dr. Foster's notes, Dr. Edwards told the nurse to prep Maggie for surgery.

The operation was routine, and Richard sat with her in the recovery room. The next day, Maggie moved to a private room on the surgical wing. Richard stopped by over his lunch hour and again that evening to see her.

Maggie had plenty of time to think while she lay in bed. That Thursday evening, she began to think about the bank. She felt the other employees didn't accept her, and she realized how much she missed the girls at Crosswell. She felt anxious about when she could use her education. Still, Miss Cooper had paid for her training at the bank so that she could earn a living and manage her affairs. But couldn't she earn a living by teaching?

Richard came in about eight o'clock, sat down, and held her hand. To him, Maggie looked gorgeous, even in the grey hospital gown. How long would he be able to hide his true feelings for her? He was content with his life, just the way it was, but this girl kept interrupting his thoughts, even while he was working.

Suddenly, without warning, Maggie began to cry. Her words tumbled out between sobs. "Richard, I don't want to stay at the bank. I want to teach. I want to teach little children like Julie's three. I want to belong. Do I have to stay at the bank?"

Richard put his arms around her. "No, no,

Maggie, you don't have to stay at the bank. You can give your notice as soon as you're out of the hospital. When Dr. Edwards releases you, apply at the school superintendent's office and maybe you can substitute until there is an opening. The bank will still look after your money for you." He smoothed her hair and held her a few minutes longer.

After a few minute, Maggie seemed more at ease. "What about Miss Cooper wanting me to stay at the bank?"

Richard reassured her. "She would want you to be happy, Maggie. Give it a go. You can always go back to the bank, if you aren't happy teaching. If you don't try, you'll always wonder if you should have."

"What will Mr. Dawson say?"

"Dawson's your attorney, not your guardian. Just send him and Mr. Charlesworth a letter that you're leaving the bank effective two weeks from the date. Tell Charlesworth you might come back in a year or two, but are returning to teaching in the meantime."

A moment or two later, Dr. Edwards came into Maggie's room and saw that she had been crying.

"Is something hurting you, Maggie? Is that why you are crying?"

"No, sir. I was feeling sad about my work, and Richard has been helping me. I'll be okay now."

Dr. Edwards patted Maggie's hand and said, "I'm glad Richard is helping you. No driving for two weeks and eat only foods which agree with you. Have you a relative who can stay with you for a week or so?"

Richard spoke up. "I'll be helping Maggie. She has no relatives nearby." Richard bent down and kissed her cheek, and then walked out with Dr. Edwards.

At noon the next day, when Richard came to visit Maggie, she was full of questions. "Can I still paint Julie's kitchen when I get home? I bought the yellow paint and the curtain material."

"No, Maggie, you can't paint anytime soon. I'll finish the kitchen while you make the curtains. I'll set up your sewing machine for you in the dining room and bring the measurements for the windows." He paused a moment, then asked, "Do you feel better about leaving the bank, Maggie?"

"I think so, but how am I going to repay you? You have been so kind to me, and I really don't have any close friends. I believe Bertha Gallaway is my friend, though."

"We're friends, Maggie, and friends don't keep accounting books." He smiled at her worried frown. "I'll take you home on Saturday."

Maggie dropped off to sleep, relieved that she didn't have to work at the bank any more.

Chapter 16

Two weeks after her surgery, Maggie phoned Richard at the hospital.

"I'm going to the bank and tell Mr. Charlesworth that I'm leaving and then I will go by Mr. Dawson's office and tell him."

"Have you contacted the school administration to see if there is an opening?"

"Yes, we talked by phone, and guess what! The second grade teacher at Lincoln Elementary is on maternity leave for the rest of the year. Mr. Martin, the principal, said I can begin on Monday." She hesitated, then asked, "Can you come over this evening, Richard?"

"Wild horses couldn't keep me away. Sure I'll come, and, Maggie, take it easy for the rest of the day. We'll have dinner at some nice place and you can tell me what Dawson and Charlesworth said when you told them the news."

"All right, Richard. About what time will you get here?"

"About five or so. I'll bring some wine and we'll celebrate."

"Richard, Miss Cooper …"

"Maggie, she isn't here anymore. Relax. Even the Good Book says a little wine is good for your stomach. I promise you, a small glass will be good for you. It didn't hurt you before, did it?"

"No, but Miss Cooper …"

"Maggie!" Richard's voice was half teasing,

half serious. "I'm not going to get you drunk, for Pete's sake. Just a small glass, a very small glass."

She took a deep breath. "Well, all right, then ... just a small glass."

"'Bye till five," Richard said, and they hung up their phones.

Never mind what Richard said. Miss Cooper's lectures about drinking popped into Maggie's mind.

Drinking, Margaret, in any form, can lead to ruin. One small glass sometimes leads to another. Alcohol loosens one's inhibitions and people say and do things, which, if they were sober, they would never dream of doing. I've never tasted any alcoholic beverage.

Maggie could almost see Miss Cooper in her tea length black Sunday dress with a prim white collar, talking about the evils of liquor. She and Maggie had been preparing the girls' Sunday breakfast, as the cook had Sunday off. Sometimes on Sundays, the girls went into town for dinner in a nice restaurant, so that Miss Cooper could instill table manners. Maggie smiled at the memory, went upstairs to make her bed, and then down to the kitchen again to fix her breakfast.

Immediately after she finished her toast and tea, she called Mr. Charlesworth's office and learned he would be available at one o'clock. To her relief, he did not seem surprised that she wanted to leave the bank.

"If your heart is in teaching, Miss Monahan, that's what you should do. After all, Miss Cooper was an educator, wasn't she? She would be proud that you have chosen to follow in her footsteps after making an honest effort to fulfill her wishes about banking."

"She wanted me to learn money management so I wouldn't be ..." Maggie hesitated a moment ... "poor."

"You'll do fine, Miss Monahan. Mr. Peters in our trust department will look after your funds and help you with investments. You don't strike me as a young lady who buys on impulse, and you already have your home paid for. So, let us manage your money while you help to educate the next generation. I'll instruct Peters as to your accounts and the bank will send you monthly statements when we send your checking account statement. I wish the very best for you."

With that, Maggie shook hands with him, and walked resolutely to the elevator.

It was a lovely Monday afternoon and she walked the four blocks to Mr. Dawson's office.

His secretary remembered her. "Good afternoon, Miss Monahan, what can we do for you today?"

"I need to speak with Mr. Dawson, please. It will only take a few minutes. I can wait."

Dawson's secretary flipped the switch on the intercom. "Miss Monahan is here.

Maggie heard him say, "Send her in." When she stepped into his office, Mr. Dawson rose and came around the desk to shake her hand.

"Miss Monahan, I heard you have been ill. How are you feeling?"

"Much better, thank you, Mr. Dawson. It was an emergency appendectomy."

"And how may I help you today, Miss Monahan?"

"I want to leave the bank and return to teaching. There's an opening at Lincoln Elementary. I will fill in for the second grade teacher who is on maternity leave." Maggie continued before he could speak. "I know this must be a disappointment, but I don't enjoy working at the bank. I want to teach. Mr. Charlesworth assures me the bank will manage my funds and send monthly statements. I know Miss Cooper wanted me to learn banking, but I always thought I would teach at Crosswell. That's what I really wanted to do." Maggie's voice trailed as if she were gathering courage for anything Mr. Dawson might say in reply.

Dawson leaned closer across the desk. "I think Miss Cooper sensed that Crosswell would be sold and that there would be no teaching job for you. She told me a little about your life before Crosswell, and she felt you had a fear of not having enough money."

"Well, that's true, Mr. Dawson. I remember that sometimes I went to bed hungry, and we moved around a lot. Some of the houses were cold in the winter and very hot in the summer."

"That's all behind you, Miss Monahan. I don't know if you are aware, but the tax bills on the duplex come to my office and Miss Cooper asked that copies of your bank statements also come to me. I'll be your trustee until you're 25, Miss Monahan. By that time, you'll be well prepared to be on your own."

"That's fine, Mr. Dawson. Whatever Miss Cooper wanted suits me."

94

"You have two brothers as I recall. Should they try to locate you after all these years, it would be best if you didn't advance them large sums of money, but rather call my office. We can direct them to where to find services and possible employment, should they wish to settle near you."

"I haven't heard from either of them, Mr. Dawson, not in all the years I lived at Crosswell or since I left there."

"Relatives have a way of showing up when they are desperate and need money, Miss Monahan, or maybe just to renew family ties. It will be easy to find you once they contact Crosswell and learn the school has been closed."

Maggie tugged nervously on the strap of her purse. "I don't believe they have any way of knowing about Crosswell. I can't imagine them looking for me anyway. Neither one of them ever paid much attention to me. They were gone a lot and when I went to Crosswell, they had been gone from home about a year."

"Just give me a call if you have any difficulty of any kind, Miss Monahan. I am always at your disposal. And good luck with your second graders. Miss Cooper would be proud of you."

Dawson rose from his desk, walked around it, and shook hands with Maggie, then ushered her to the door.

Maggie went straight home, hung up her suit jacket, and began to think of her brothers. It was difficult to remember much of anything about them.

"Oh well," she thought as she went into the kitchen to make a cup of tea, "that's the least of my worries. Right now, I have to decide what to wear to dinner. I don't have anything to wear to a really nice place."

The doorbell rang. Richard stood at the door, six yellow roses in his hand. He handed these to Maggie, and they walked into the kitchen.

Chapter 17

Maggie and Richard celebrated at the Savoy Hotel restaurant, one of the oldest in Davenport. They didn't need reservations, as the restaurant catered mostly to business people and other professionals.

"Let me order for you tonight, Maggie. The Savoy has the best petite steaks, just the right size. They serve a medium sized baked potato, and we'll get a house salad." The waiter moved quickly to their table and stood there.

"That's fine, Richard."

After he ordered for them, and the waiter moved away, Richard asked how her appointments had gone.

She gave a brief account of her meeting with Mr. Charlesworth at the bank, then moved on to her meeting with the attorney.

"They both wished me well. Then Mr. Dawson asked me about my brothers and hinted that one or both of them would come to me for money. How does he know my brothers? I haven't even thought of them for a long time … maybe just once or twice when I first went to Crosswell."

"He has your files," Richard reminded her. "Lawyers hear things and see records that we don't. He may have run across your brothers' names in connection with some case. It's not beyond the realm of possibility."

"Why would Mr. Dawson be worried if they ask me for money?"

"Well, Maggie, I don't know, but what about

your brothers? I don't ever remember you even mentioning them. What are their names and how old are they?"

"Well, let's see. Kenny and Joey were 15 and 16 when I went to Crosswell, but they were gone a lot before that. Sometimes they wouldn't be home for maybe a week and then they'd come back home. I think they went to school some. That was 12 years ago. They would be about 27 and 28 now."

"What kind of kids were they? Did they have part time jobs?"

"Jobs? I don't think so. They fought with Mama a lot, and Daddy, too but mostly Daddy. They got into trouble at school and I believe they dropped out. I'm not sure, actually. I don't remember them very well. When I was real little, they would tease me."

"Is it fair to judge them, Maggie? Who knows, maybe they straightened out and started a business, are partners and get along fine."

"What about Mama and Daddy, Richard? I haven't heard a word from them either, not since I went to Crosswell. That's how Miss Cooper became my guardian."

"Like you, I haven't the foggiest notion of where your folks are, Maggie, but it does seem strange that all four of them would drop out of sight. It seems as if Crosswell would have heard something. But, Maggie, just cross that bridge when you come to it."

"Mr. Dawson said if either of my brothers came and asked me for money, I should let him … I mean Mr. Dawson … know and he would help them find work."

They finished the meal and lingered over coffee.

"Dawson probably knows something that you don't and doesn't want to worry you. Anyhow, if they come to town, either one or both, or your parents, for that matter, just give me a call. It's not a good idea to let people know that you're alone, and you really aren't, Maggie. You have me." Richard reached over and covered her hand with his.

Maggie smiled at him. "I feel so much better after I told you this about my brothers. I promise I will call you immediately if I hear from them."

"Good. Maggie, you don't carry more than ten or twenty dollars in cash with you, do you?"

"Sometimes I draw out a hundred in cash to last me through the month for gas and incidentals. Sometimes more. I buy groceries for cash also, and the paper boy."

"Start writing checks, Maggie. To the grocery store, the gas station, the cleaners, and other places where you trade regularly. Draw twenty in cash when you need it. Use your credit card for big purchases."

"My credit card! Richard, I hate debt! Mama and Daddy were always fighting about money ... how much they owed." Maggie stopped talking and looked at Richard as if she had been caught in a lie.

"Maggie, Maggie, you'll be okay. Miss Cooper taught you well. What did she say about debt?"

"That it was dishonorable to owe money, and that when you contracted for something, it was a debt of honor to be paid immediately, at least within 30 days. She thought bankruptcy was tantamount to stealing."

"Debt is a tool, Maggie. It's like everything else. It can be a good thing if not abused." He changed the subject. "Want some dessert?"

"No, thank you, Richard. I'm so excited about starting school on Monday. I can hardly wait. I'll probably forget all about Mr. Dawson and my brothers." Maggie wiped her lips with the linen napkin. "They have certainly forgotten about me."

Richard motioned to the waiter for the check, then he drove Maggie home. There, he kissed her goodnight, then listened for her to lock the door before driving away.

Chapter 18

Maggie's first day at school was one of pure joy. She made nametags for each of her second graders, knew right away which of the boys would be the 'vitamin kids' and the girls to whom she would be forever telling, 'no talking in class'. Maggie inspected the miniature restroom attached to her classroom and satisfied herself that it was neat and clean, checked the paper towels in the child-sized holder, and then closed the door and walked to her desk.

There was one little girl who reminded her of herself when she was little, Carla with her dark eyes holding too much sadness for one so small. She wore faded clothes, yet she appeared eager to learn. As Maggie walked by, she noted how hard Carla pressed the pencil onto her paper as she printed her spelling words. At recess, Martha, her teacher aide, took the kids to the playground. Maggie looked in Carla's desk. She had placed a tablet with a large coffee stain on it neatly on her desk shelf. With it was a spelling book and reader, which the district provided. Three stubby pencils, one with an eraser, lay alongside the books.

Carla was one of the 'hot lunch children', as Maggie discovered when she lined the children up for lunch. Carla clutched her yellow ticket tightly and, after getting her tray, sat by herself at the end of a table reserved for second graders. None of the other kids came to sit by her.

Maggie decided in that moment that she must learn more about Carla and see what help she needed.

On her way home that evening, Maggie thought aloud, "I mustn't get too involved. I need to see what she needs and try to get it. The poor little girl appears not to have any friends. She must be new in the district. I'd better talk to Miss Johnson about her before class tomorrow."

When Maggie opened her mail that evening, she found two letters. One was postmarked 'Little Falls, Wyoming'. The Crosswell address was marked out with black marker and her Lombard street address neatly affixed to the envelope. Maggie turned over the letter. There was no return address. She didn't know anyone in Wyoming. She looked at the address again. The letter had been forwarded from Crosswell by the post office. Her hand trembled as she opened the one page note. It was from her brother, Kenny.

'Dear, Maggie, I remembered you were at Crosswell. I ran into Mom a year or so ago, and she told me they sent you there. Don't know where Joey is. Mom or Dad either. They must be bumming around the country hoping for a gig. I'm broke … last deal didn't turn out too good, but I'm heading south … see you soon … soon as I can hitch a ride. Your long lost brother, Kenny.'

Maggie took the letter to the kitchen, left it on the counter, put her teakettle on to boil for tea, and called Richard.

He listened while Maggie read the letter.

"Do you want me to come over and we can talk about the letter, Maggie?

"No, but could I come over to your house?"

"Of course you can! And, Maggie, drive carefully."

"I will, Richard, and thank you."

Maggie shut off the stove burner and drove to Richard's condo. She hurried into the lobby, her heart racing as she pressed the bell. She clutched the letter in her hand as the elevator took her to the third floor. Richard opened the door and motioned for her to come in.

When he saw her hurried breathing, he said, "Take it easy, Maggie. Take it easy." He held her briefly.

Before Maggie sat down, she looked into Richard's eyes and asked anxiously, "How did Mr. Dawson know?"

Richard motioned her to the sofa and sat down beside her, then slipped his arm around her shoulders. "Lawyers hear things and read records to which we don't have access, Maggie. It might just be a coincidence. After all, Dawson had lots of conversations with Miss Cooper when you first went to Crosswell. He knew all about your mom and dad taking off and that your brothers had already gone."

"But do you think Kenny did something … that's he's hiding from the law or something?"

"Don't borrow trouble, Maggie. Let's read the letter again."

They scanned it, then Richard broke the silence. "The letter says a lot. Your brother has no money and he plans to stay with you for a while and possibly hopes you'll stake him to whatever venture he's planning."

"Well, I do have the spare bedroom where he can sleep. I can give him some money to start over until he finds a job."

"Whoa, Maggie. Not so fast. Remember Dawson's warning about calling his office?" He laid the letter on the table.

Maggie persisted. "Mr. Dawson must know something, Richard. I'm sure of it."

"I'll make coffee, Maggie, then we'll get some dinner." When he returned, Maggie had taken the letter and was smoothing it out on her lap. He took the letter from her and held her hand. "Maggie, what do you think of this plan. Tomorrow, draw out any money from your account except what you'll need for the week and then see what your brother needs. Then you can plan and see if you can help him."

"But, Richard, I have Miss Cooper's money she left me, and I've been saving my salary from the bank and the hospital, and I don't pay rent ..."

"He doesn't need to know that, Maggie. See what he needs and then decide. It's not a good idea to tell your relatives, or anyone else for that matter, about your finances."

"If Kenny comes, will you come over, too, Richard?"

"If you'd like me to, Maggie, sure I will. If your brother shows up, call me. Now, today's Wednesday, and you have two days before the weekend. If Kenny shows up on your doorstep, invite him in and call me. We'll go to dinner at one of those chain steak houses.

Everybody wears informal duds to those places. We can sound him out about his plans there."

"I don't know how soon he'll get here, but, okay, when he comes, I'll invite him in and then call you."

"Now, let's go get something to eat, then you can sleep on it. Tomorrow, things will straighten out and I'll help you get through whatever comes."

They had dinner at Julie's café, and when Maggie got home, she put the letter in Miss Cooper's desk and went to bed.

Chapter 19

Thursday and Friday seemed literally to fly. On Friday at four o'clock, Maggie locked her second grade room and walked to the parking lot. On the way home, she thought of Carla. Miss Johnson, the principal, told Maggie that Carla was one of the migrant worker's children and that the family had moved into the area this school year. There were six other children in the family. Carla was the oldest girl.

"I must call on the family," Maggie thought. "Maybe Carla needs a few more clothes. I could get some for her at the Salvation Army. Maybe one or two new pieces thrown in … maybe some new shoes and socks and underwear. It seems as if underwear was never donated."

Maggie pulled into her driveway, and there was her brother sitting on the steps. Maggie was sure it was Kenny. She remembered his dark brown wavy hair that he was always pushing out of his face.

"Hi, Maggie. Found you in the phone book over at the gas station where I got let out. You're lookin' good." He came closer and gave Maggie a hug. They walked into the duplex together.

Kenny flopped into the nearest chair. "Nice digs ya' got here, sis! How much does the rent set you back? Who's the guy next door? He gave me the once over real good before I told him I was your brother."

"That's Mr. Scott. He does the outside maintenance. He was here when I came. He washes windows, mows and things like that."

Maggie turned towards the stairs. "Kenny, I'm going to run upstairs and change. I'll be right down. We're going out to dinner with a friend of mine. I didn't have any idea when you would get here, so I didn't fix anything. We're going to one of those chain steak houses."

"Okay. I'll be right here, Sis."

Maggie changed into her brown slacks with a beige turtleneck top. She placed a quick call to Richard then returned downstairs. When she sat down on the sofa, Kenny's questions began.

"What happened at the school where the judge put you? When I went by there the sign was gone. Looks like they're adding on. Lots of heavy equipment sittin' around."

"Crosswell was sold. The heirs sold it to a developer. There are going to be several houses on the ten acres. I think they're going to call it 'Crosswell Estates'. Probably use the mansion as the office complex." She glanced toward the front window, hoping to see Richard's car pulling in.

"So, how long ya' been here, sis?" Kenny asked, putting his cigarette out in a candy dish. Maggie wanted to tell him she didn't like anyone smoking in the house, but she couldn't.

"I've been here since Miss Cooper died. She was superintendent at Crosswell. She taught all the grades through eighth grade and then we went on to high school."

"You must have gone to college, beings that you're a teacher. Where did you get the bucks,

Maggie?"

She hesitated for a moment before answering Kenny. Maggie thought about what Richard said about telling relatives everything about finances. Mr. Dawson had said much the same thing. Her mind raced for an answer. She swallowed briefly and then said calmly, "I went to Capitol University on a scholarship." I went on Miss Cooper's money, Maggie thought, and that's the same thing as a scholarship.

Maggie wasn't prepared for Kenny's next question. "Did this friend we're going to dinner with set you up in this place?"

"Set me up? I don't know what you mean."

"Yeah, you do. Is he paying for these fancy digs?"

Just then she saw Richard pull into the driveway. Thank God, she said silently and went to open the door.

Kenny rose when Richard entered.

Chapter 20

Maggie introduced them. "Richard, I'd like you to meet my brother, Kenny. Kenny, Richard Allen." The two men shook hands. Maggie said, "Let's go. I'm famished. I only had an apple and a half sandwich for lunch."

All three slid their trays down the menu line. All three ordered the buffet. Richard chose a medium steak, as did Kenny, while Maggie ordered a petite cut. Kenny filled his plate with macaroni and cheese, beans and mashed potatoes with gravy. Richard and Maggie chose baked potatoes with a green salad. All three took coffee.

Maggie figured that, as long as they concentrated on food, she wouldn't have to answer any questions. However, Kenny began the conversation the moment they were seated.

"You a teacher, too, Richard?"

"No. I'm in the Pathology Department at the hospital."

"I worked at a hospital once, pushing people in wheelchairs all over the place. No money, so I quit. You a tech of some kind?"

"No. I'm the pathologist."

"You an MD? Like a doctor?"

"Yes, I took my training at Yale Medical."

Kenny was impressed. "Wow! Graduate of Yale! No wonder you can keep Maggie on Lombard Street."

Richard put his fork down and looked at Kenny.

"Let's get this straight, Ken. Maggie takes care of herself and conducts her own business. You insult your sister when you assume I'm keeping her." He sipped his coffee, then continued, "And, Sport, if I were keeping her it would be none of your business. Now, let's enjoy our meal."

They continued eating in silence. Kenny cleaned his plate and then went to the dessert bar where he took a large slice of apple pie and put soft ice cream on top. He refilled his coffee cup and went back to the booth. Richard and Maggie declined dessert, and they soon left the restaurant.

When they reached Maggie's duplex, Richard walked to the door with them.

"I'll see you in the morning, Maggie," Richard said. "I'll come by and we'll go out for breakfast. You're welcome to come, too, Kenny."

"No thanks, I'm bushed. I'll probably sleep till noon. You two go ahead. Good night."

Kenny went into the living room and stretched out on the sofa, closed his eyes and went to sleep instantly.

Maggie whispered to Richard in the hallway. "I don't think he has anything."

"Don't worry, Maggie. Things will work out." He held her close, kissed her goodnight and walked to his car.

Maggie watched from the doorway until his lights disappeared.

***

The next morning, as soon as Richard and Maggie pulled out of the driveway, Kenny got up, yawned, and went to the kitchen to pour a cup of coffee, which Maggie had brewed for him before she left.

While he was in the shower, he decided to call Crystal, an old girlfriend from his high school days ... that is when he showed up for class. He'd called her off and on through the years, learned she had been married, divorced with no kids, and was working at the courthouse in the tax office. It was time to call her again.

When he dialed the familiar number, Crystal answered in a sleepy voice, "Yeah, what do you want and why? I ain't got it."

"Crystal," came the deep familiar voice of Kenny Monahan, "it's your true love. I'm hangin' out with my sister, Maggie. Over on Lombard Street."

"Lombard Street? She must have a few bucks. That's right up close to Millionaire's Row. She renting there?"

"I don't know. She hasn't come right out and said so, but there's this guy who lives in the other half of the duplex ... he mows and stuff ... I don't know what the deal is. I thought if you looked up the taxes on the place, we could figure out about what rent they're paying."

"Why would you need to know that, Kenny?"

"I'm fixin' to borrow a few bucks to start my club."

"Club? What club? Kenny, how are you going

to start a club? You've got to pay rent on a building, buy inventory, hire help, pay the utilities. It's going to cost you at least five thousand for starting costs."

"Well, that's where Maggie comes in, darlin'. I borrow the five thou from her and presto, I rent a building down on Front Street, buy whatever inventory the owners have. The Front Street Tavern is for sale. Gotta sell forty percent of my inventory in food sales. Then I can get a dancin' license."

"How do you know she's got five thousand laying around and even if she has, will she loan it to you?"

"I've been thinkin', Crystal, darlin' … didn't that head woman at Crosswell die suddenly in an accident in London? Couple years ago, maybe?"

Crystal interrupted. "Do you think she left Maggie some money? Wait a minute … just a damn minute. There's a new clerk over in the clerk's office. That's where the wills and stuff are kept. I know she came from Crosswell, because that social worker who was with her had her apply at the Treasurer's office, but we didn't have any openings. Let's see her name is … oh hell, that doesn't matter, Kenny. I'll find out her name and have her look up the will. What was the head teacher's name? I don't remember, but she will … no … it's better that I look it up and see what the will says. Say, Kenny, whatcha doing the rest of the day?"

"Not much. Maggie and her boyfriend are going to the Iowa-Michigan basketball game. I'm free as a bird. What did you have in mind, darlin'?"

"Well, I'll come by and get you, and we'll go get some breakfast, cruise down on Front Street and look the place over. Maybe go in this afternoon and have a few beers."

"Sounds, great, darlin'. I'll drag on my one and only pair of jeans and be ready in about twenty minutes. I'll watch for you."

"Okay, and Kenny ... I've put on a pound or two since we met up in Vegas last year. Getting' old, I guess."

"More of you to love, darlin'."

Crystal Lewis fit the description of a blowsy blonde. Bottle Blonde. She was twenty pounds overweight and wore her clothes too tight to be flattering. She was fond of Bud, or any brand, for that matter, and a whiz with the calculator. Her fingers could race over the keys, with her eyes never leaving the pages of figures she was adding. She knew the percentages for tax mileage and could figure a patron's taxes faster than any other clerk in the Treasurer's Office, where she had worked since she graduated from high school.

Crystal drove up and Kenny came out of Maggie's duplex, dressed in a faded flannel shirt and well-worn jeans."

"Hi, Crystal darlin', glad to see me?"

"Sure am, Kenny. Let's chow down and we'll go explorin'."

They drove to Front Street Diner, about two blocks north of the tavern. The tablecloths were red and white checked. A small white vase of artificial flowers decorated each table. There was only one waitress, who smiled as she came to get their order.

"Bacon and eggs, a biscuit and gravy for me," Kenny said before Crystal could order. "Same for you, darlin'?

"Heck no," Crystal said indignantly. "It's too early for all that food. Coffee, orange juice, and an English muffin, please." Crystal smiled at the waitress and folded her napkin in her lap.

"Hey," Kenny said. "I forgot to leave Maggie a note."

"Well, don't sweat it, Kenny, darlin', we'll stick one in her mailbox when we leave here. I've always got paper and pen in my purse."

In ten minutes, the waitress brought their order and Kenny almost smacked his lips. The food smelled delicious.

After breakfast, they drove by Maggie's and Kenny placed a note in her mailbox.

"Dear Maggie. Met up with an old friend. We're going to look over a business deal I've got in mind. Is it okay if I bring her over for supper? Her name is Crystal. See you soon. Kenny. PS, Be home at six o'clock."

Chapter 21

On Wednesday, Crystal went into the Clerk's office in the courthouse and found Mary Pat at her desk. Crystal didn't need to ask which one was the girl from Crosswell, as she remembered Mary Pat wore thick glasses and had long black hair, which she kept putting behind her ear.

Crystal stopped at her desk. "Hi, Mary Pat, remember me? I'm Crystal from the Treasurer's Office. You came to apply for a job there a while back, but we didn't have any openings."

"I think I remember you, but I'm not sure. Can I help you with something?"

"You sure can. I need to look at the will of Miss Cooper ... Miss Rachel ..."

"Yes, I know. I've been gone from Crosswell about a year and a half. That's when Miss Cooper died. Car accident in London. Wait here and I'll get it."

Crystal hesitated a moment before adding, "Lombard Street is next to Millionaire's Row, isn't it? That's where Miss Cooper's duplex is."

"Lombard Street is located on Cooper farmland. Miss Cooper's dad owned a large farm where Lombard Street is now. Some 500 acres, which is a lot of land in the city."

"Yeah, a lot of land," Crystal said. "It must have sold for big bucks."

"Something like $3,000 an acre," Mary Pat added as she walked into the vault where the wills were kept.

Crystal almost grabbed the will from Mary Pat's hand.

Mary Pat didn't seem to mind and invited Crystal to sit at a small table by the door.

Crystal scanned the will hastily. "Yep," she thought, "the old gal left everything to Maggie. Probably didn't need to spend a dime of her inheritance because Miss Cooper got free room and board along with her job at Crosswell."

"Mary Pat, can I have a copy of this will?"

"Sure, it's public record. It's 50 cents a page."

The will was only three pages with lots of white space, leaving everything to Maggie. Crystal dug into her purse and found a dollar and a half in change. She had another idea. "Mary Pat, can you get me the deed from the Cooper farm to the buyer?"

"Okay, do you want a copy of that, too?"

"No, just the amount and the developer or people who bought the land.

"Okay." Mary Pat came back with the deed book. The Cooper deed was recorded in book 95, page 46.

Crystal was impatient. "How much?"

"Cooper Farm to Davenport Development, $1,500,000."

"What was the date?"

"1950."

Crystal looked over Mary Pat's shoulder. "Probably she gave a bunch to charity."

"There's no way of knowing that," Mary Pat

said.

"The will just gives Maggie all of Miss Cooper's assets."

Crystal took the copy of the will with her, went back to her office, and began her filing. When she saw Kenny, the next thing on the program was to find out if Maggie would part with any of her money. Especially to buy a tavern or club, as Kenny so grandly put it.

Chapter 22

That evening, Crystal called Kenny at Maggie's house.

Kenny answered the phone, flopping down on the living room sofa. "Monahan residence, Maggie's brother speaking."

"Well, hi, Maggie's brother. Got great news, well, maybe great news. Maggie got all of Miss Cooper's assets, whatever that means, plus the duplex, her cash, stocks and bonds, her car and all the household furnishing that Maggie's got in her duplex. Looks like Maggie's been getting a free ride."

"I'll leave Maggie a note and meet you at Mama Maria's. I've got a taste for Italian spaghetti with sausage and that sauce they make. A little wine to go along with the dinner. Okay? By the way, I've run out of cash … can you handle dinner?"

"Okay, Kenny, but remember, I'm not Maggie. I haven't got near her moola. I'm just a working gal. Takes almost every dime, but I will get a pension if I stay with the county and then I'll get Social Security. I'm not much on saving … life's too short … hell, I may get hit by a truck tomorrow."

"Yeah, yeah, Crystal … you got more than I have, so I'll meet you in about 20 minutes. Wait, you come and get me. Maggie isn't home yet, and I don't have any wheels."

"Okay, Kenny, I'll be by. You be on the front steps when I come. I hate waiting for people."

"Bye for now, Crystal, darlin'."

Kenny set the kitchen timer to be sure he was ready when Crystal came. Sure enough, she was right on time, so Kenny piled into her car and they went to Mama Maria's.

They had hardly sat down when Crystal began. "Look, Kenny, I didn't know this Miss Cooper. I never was in the joint. I don't know what she told Maggie about money, or for that matter, about life. If I was you, I wouldn't bank on Maggie parting with any of her money. The old lady might have put strings on it." Crystal paused, then continued. "How old is Maggie? She got a boyfriend? Does he live with her?"

"She's about 24, I think … she's got a boyfriend. At least, I think he's a boyfriend although he got right riled when I hinted they were living together. He's a pathologist at the hospital. That's where they met, when Maggie was working there."

"Have you said anything to Maggie about this club you want to start? Has she looked at this place you want to buy? Has she got a clue as to why you came back, Kenny?"

"No, I figure this weekend, Sis and I will have a little talk. I'll tell her I've been driftin' long enough, and I want to settle down, get married and have kids … have a business. I want to be my own boss."

"Sounds great, Kenny. Who do you figure on marryin'?"

"Well, you, of course, Crystal. I'm not getting down on my knees or nothin' like that, but that's what I'm fixin' to do. I figure we can get married by a JP. Maggie won't care … she's not into frills."

"Yeah." Crystal smiled at the waiter when he brought her place. "I want to invite my girlfriend from work. No justice of the peace, though. We can get married in the Methodist Chapel, just a small room, not the big church. My cousin Sam got married there and all he did was pay the preacher $50.00. Maggie might spring for a suit for you. Then I want to go to a restaurant and have dinner. We can live in my apartment until you get your tavern, uh, I mean club."

"Okay. Say, this chow is great! You cook, darlin'?"

"Well, in a way. I can do eggs, make spaghetti, fry hamburgers. But heck anybody can cook if they can read."

They finished the meal and topped it off with a glass of wine. Crystal left a $2.00 tip and they drove to Maggie's duplex, where her car was parked in the driveway.

Chapter 23

Kenny bounded up the steps to Maggie's duplex, turned the door handle and hollered in. "Hi, Maggie, it's Kenny and I've brought Crystal."

Maggie came from the kitchen, wiping her hands on the kitchen towel. "Hello, you two. Have you had supper?"

"Yeah, we already ate. Got some great news, Maggie!" Kenny put his arm around Crystal's waist and hugged her. "Maggie, meet your soon-to-be new sister-in-law. Crystal has said 'yes' and we're getting hitched."

Maggie hugged Crystal briefly and murmured, "Congratulations. When is the wedding, and where?"

Crystal looked up at Kenny, her eyes glowing. "We're getting married in the Methodist Chapel on Weaver Street next Saturday. I know Reverend Walker real good ... he married my cousin Sammy. You're comin', ain't cha?"

"Of course. I'll have to get a new dress. Come on into the kitchen ... there's coffee left ... and tell me about your plans."

Crystal began. "I'm inviting some of my girlfriends from work and Kenny's got a pal or two he knew in high school. They'll bring wives, of course, then we want to go and dance. You'll bring that doctor guy who hangs around, won't cha, Maggie?"

"Richard will be happy to come. Where do you plan to live?"

Kenny took Crystal's hand. "We're gonna live

at Crystal's place until I get my apartment ready. There's an apartment over the club. Did I tell you, Maggie, I'm fixin' to buy this little club down on Front Street? I've got to have 40 percent food sales to get a dancin' license. There's this guy I know from Texas who'll come up and work for me once I get it goin'."

"Do you have some money saved, Kenny? I thought you were without funds."

"Not exactly, Maggie. I figure you could give me a grubstake in this place, for a percentage of the profits." Kenny stood up, walked to the counter and poured himself more coffee. He waved his hand in the air as he sat down. "We'll work out the details, and when Crystal and I get back from doin' stuff, you and me can hammer out the deal."

"How much money does this 'grubstake' as you call it, involve, Kenny?"

"I figure about five thousand dollars. Down payment on the business and the first thee month's rent on the building. I'll need to buy the owner's inventory. The joint needs painting and some fixin' up."

Crystal interrupted. "And yeah, anything I have anything to do with has got to be clean ... real clean ... I want the john to have white tiles on the wall at least part way and a new floor and new plumbing. The john tells you as much about a place as anything. Don't you agree, Maggie?"

"Oh yes, any public eating place should have a clean rest room. Miss Cooper..."

Maggie stopped mid-sentence, picked up her

cup and drank … Miss Cooper wouldn't be caught dead in a tavern. Maggie finished her coffee. "I quote Miss Cooper too often, but she made a great impression on me. At Crosswell, the housekeeper cleaned everything, especially the restrooms, every day! Even the floors were scrubbed each day."

"Wow," Crystal said. "That is clean, but I'll bet the club's floors will have to be scrubbed every day. People use the potty a lot when they're drinkin'."

Crystal and Kenny put their cups on the counter and went to the front door. "See you this evening, Maggie," Kenny said. "And have the doc come over. He's probably advising you on how to spend that dough the old lady left you. Crystal got a copy of the will. See ya."

Crystal and Kenny got into Crystal's car and roared off. Their first stop was the tavern for sale on Front Street.

Chapter 24

After Crystal and Kenny left, Maggie sat down at the kitchen table, folding and refolding a napkin. She was thinking of Miss Cooper, who had very firm ideas about alcohol, dancing and so-called nightlife. Maggie could almost hear her.

Liquor, Margaret, is very bad. It dulls the senses and causes one to do and say things, which a sober person would never say or do. Dancing could lead to immorality ... not folk dancing, reels and polkas and such, but when people hold each other very closely ... it is not the thing for young women of breeding to do, even though I admit some do.

Maggie thought about what Miss Cooper would say if anyone asked her for money for anything. Again, her voice seems to come out of the grave.

Margaret, never lend money to friends or relatives. It causes hard feelings. You could lend a cup of sugar or almost anything else, but money, no. If the occasion should arise and you have to loan money to a relative, only in dire circumstances, a medical reason for instance, always get a signed note stating when and how that person will repay the money.

No, Maggie thought, getting up to load the dishwasher, I couldn't loan Kenny any of Miss Cooper's money, but I could loan him some of mine. I have five thousand in savings and revenue from the rental house. I have so much and Kenny and Crystal are just starting out. If I lend them my money, then it will be okay. I'd better call Richard. She dialed him from the kitchen phone.

"Hello, Richard, this is Maggie. It seems as if I always need you for something! Could you come over around seven? Kenny will be home, I expect around eight. He wants to buy a tavern down on Front Street."

"Where did he get the money? I thought he was broke."

"That's the problem. He wants to borrow five thousand from me. I'd only lend him my money, Richard, not Miss Cooper's. She never held with drinking or dancing, and Kenny wants to open this place and do both of those things."

"I'll be over, Maggie. Don't do anything until I get there. It helps to talk it over with someone before making such a decision. Were you planning to talk it over with your lawyer?"

"Oh, no. Mr. Dawson would never agree to that. I don't think he likes my brothers."

"Well, I'll be over in a little while and then we will talk it out. That is, if you want me to help you decide."

"Of course, I do, Richard! Otherwise, I wouldn't have bothered you. You've been so good to me; you're really my best friend. Oh, I forgot to tell you that Kenny and Crystal are getting married Saturday in the Methodist Chapel. They're going to a club afterward to have dinner and dance. I don't know if I should go. Miss Cooper ..."

Richard interrupted her. "Maggie, Miss Cooper isn't here. She's a wonderful memory, but you have to decide about the money, about dancing, and everything else. I'll be there in a bit. Bye."

With that, Maggie went upstairs to change her clothes, her thoughts racing. I hope Kenny and Richard don't get mad at each other. I do want to help him, though. He is my brother. I don't think he's had it easy, not as easy as I have.

Maggie straightened the pillows on the sofa, put on a pot of coffee and waited for Richard to come. She opened the door when she saw his car pull up.

Richard kissed her briefly on the cheek and sat down in the overstuffed chair by the window. He began. "Tell me about this place Kenny wants to buy."

"It's down on Front Street. He wants to serve food so he can get a dancing license. I think he said 40 percent of his revenue from the tavern has to be in food. Crystal says it needs cleaning and some repair. She wants new plumbing and the bathrooms fixed. She says you can tell a lot about a place by the restrooms."

"True. I think you'll have to go down and inspect the place yourself, Maggie."

"What about the money, Richard? Is it okay for me to loan him my money, not any of Miss Cooper's?"

"Maggie," Richard replied, tolerance in his voice. "Miss Cooper's money *is* your money and she's not here to ask, remember?"

"I know that, Richard, but I feel so guilty about using any of her money for liquor. I feel if I did, I would be betraying her trust."

"Then don't, Maggie. Let's wait until Kenny and Crystal get here and we'll go with them and look over the place. Don't promise Kenny the money until you have taken the tour. Okay?"

"Okay, Richard. They ought to be here around eight or so."

Chapter 25

Crystal and Kenny arrived a few minutes after eight. Maggie locked her front door. Richard opened the side door of the car for Maggie, and Crystal pulled away with a squeal of tires.

The Front Street Tavern stood between a locksmith's shop and a second hand store, which sold nearly everything, from used clothing to knickknacks. The tavern had a huge plate glass window in the front, curtained half way with black café curtains. The outside door, painted a battleship gray, was badly in need of another coat of paint.

There were several patrons in the tavern. About five sat on high stools at the bar and three or four couples were nursing drinks at booths. The bar itself was walnut and badly in need of a good cleaning and polishing.

Crystal took Maggie's arm. "Let's take a tour, Maggie. As you can see, this place needs lots of soap and water from top to bottom. Look at the top of the big window ... even in the dark you can see how dirty it is. And look at the floor. Gotta rent a sander and take off all this crap on top. Then it will have to be varnished with two or three coats, doncha think?"

Maggie couldn't help but think of how Miss Cooper would have described the place. *No place for ladies or any person of breeding.* But if Miss Cooper had fallen heir to such a place, she would have thought the same as Crystal ... generous amount of soap and water before she had an agent sell the place.

Maggie agreed with Crystal, too. "It certainly needs cleaning. Will you and Kenny have a cleaning service and go to a restaurant supply house for new things for the kitchen?"

"Heck, no, Maggie. Yours truly can do all the soap and water stuff. Can't afford restaurant supply. There're secondhand places that sell all kinds of stuff we need and less than half of retail. I can make new curtains for the window. When we can afford it, me and Kenny will get new booths. You comin' to the wedding?"

"Of course, Crystal. Richard and I will be happy to come."

"You gonna loan Kenny some money. He's got nothin'... Kenny's been kind of a rover. Needs to settle down. I'm nuts about him."

"I'm happy for both of you, Crystal. We'll talk about money after we all tour this place. We can go out for coffee."

"No drinks, Maggie?"

"I don't drink, Crystal."

"A little wine won't hurt you. Here's the kitchen ... such as it is!"

Crystal went over to the sink. "This has gotta go. See the enamel is all chipped and look at these faucets. Must have been put in when the place was first built. Look at the floor, too! This linoleum ... I won't be able to get it clean! I hate dirt, Maggie. My mom always said if you're poor as dirt, you can always be clean. She was always scrubbin' something ... the floor, us kids ... scrubbin', scrubbin', scrubbin'.

Bet you did a lot of that at Miss Cooper's didn't ya? Probably worked you kids to death."

Maggie smiled, remembering her early days at Crosswell. "No, we didn't work. I went there when I was ten. We made our beds, learned 'domestic science', how to cook and iron and sew, but there was a housekeeper. I never scrubbed a floor."

"Gee," Crystal said. "I thought those places made all the kids work."

"It wasn't really an orphanage. It was more like a boarding school. The county orphanage was full, so the judge sent me to Crosswell."

"Did Kenny or Joey or your mom and dad ever visit you?"

Maggie hid her hurt. "No, not once."

"Why?"

"I don't know."

"Heck, I know Kenny needs some money, but you sure don't owe him anything. Wouldn't blame you a bit if you told him to get lost."

"But I have been given so much, Crystal. I want to share with you and Kenny. If we can reach an agreement, it will be from my personal funds, money I earned, not Miss Cooper's money. She didn't approve of drinking or dancing."

"Oh, Maggie, I can hardly wait to clean this place up and see what it looks like."

The bathroom, in Maggie's eyes, was a disaster. The floor had loose tiles, the toilet looked as if no one had ever cleaned it and a paper towel holder hung on a dark green wall with no towels in it. The washbasin had only one usable faucet; the other one had no handle.

"Ditto cleaning for the bathroom," Crystal said. "Maybe I can repair these few tiles. Soap and water will do wonders for this, too. Looks like someone painted over the window." Crystal left the light on and took Maggie's arm as they went to find Kenny and Richard.

The men had been in the basement, checking out the heating system. The furnace appeared to be fairly new and the hot water tank had a recent sticker of inspection. The water pipes overhead were fairly new also.

"Won't need a new furnace or water heater, that's for sure. Well, what do you think, Richard?" Kenny asked.

"I think you could make a go of it, Kenny. Lots of hours to say nothing of cleaning the upstairs. You probably will just break even the first year or two."

Kenny and Richard went upstairs. Maggie and Crystal were sitting in the first booth by the door. They signaled for the guys to sit down. The bartender brought beers for Crystal, Kenny and Richard, and a lemonade for Maggie.

Richard pulled out a small notebook and they began to outline the start-up costs.

Chapter 26

Maggie tried on three dresses before choosing the blue chiffon, tea length, 'can wear to church' dress. Swirls of print in deeper blue with white tips relieved the overall blue. She wore black sandals with ankle straps.

From a small jewelry box, she took out the pearls Miss Cooper had given her for her seventeenth birthday. What would she think of Crystal, and the tavern and Kenny? Well, I did get a signed note. Miss Cooper would like that. Maggie looked in the mirror one more time, and then closed the door behind her.

Richard was waiting in her living room, looking handsome in a navy pin stripe suit, white shirt and small patterned tie. He looked up as Maggie came into the room. "Hi, don't you look snazzy!"

"I had a terrible time deciding which dress. It's rather low in the neck. That's why I picked the pearls."

"You look just fine, Maggie."

***

John, Crystal's father, asked to be excused from attending breakfast, as he had stomach problems, and there were so many foods he didn't eat.

Eleanor, Crystal's mother, dismissed John's condition cheerfully and said, laughing, as she got into Richard's car: "More for me. John hates to eat out … guess I've got him spoiled."

At the restaurant, Eleanor began to question Maggie about her living arrangements. "How come you own that place, a duplex with a renter? Someone

132

leave you a bundle?"

Maggie glanced at Richard. He had almost a look of resignation on his face. She had to control her own features. "Well, Eleanor, as a matter of fact, someone did. My mentor at Crosswell left me the duplex. She had it built a few years before she died. She planned to live in it when she retired."

Eleanor put down her coffee cup. "What happened to her?"

Maggie said quietly, "She was hit by a car while crossing a street in London."

"I'm sorry to hear that," Eleanor said, and then went on. "Does this renter mow and do all that stuff ... you know, kinda keep the place up?"

"Yes, that's how Miss Cooper planned it."

"Crystal told me you made a loan to the kids. That was real nice of you. I'll tell you, Crystal will see that Kenny pays back every dime. That gal's got great credit. Just like her dad and me. Why, we hardly put the bill on the table after it's opened 'til someone wrote the check and popped it in the mail. My Crystal's a worker, too. She'll help Kenny keep that place sparklin'. I raised her right, I tell ya."

Eleanor beamed at Maggie and Richard, waved her fork in the air, and asked abruptly, "Where do you teach? I never liked kids that much, so it's a good thing I'm not a teacher. Liked my own, though, my little Crystal."

Maggie smiled at Eleanor. "I teach the second grade. The school is about four blocks away from my home."

"You gotta car? Winters get mighty cold here in the Midwest."

"Yes, I have a car. Miss Cooper left it to me."

Before Eleanor could ask another question, Richard said, "Is John retired?"

"Oh, yes, he sure is, loafs around the house all day. Likes to drive though. I hate to drive so he hauls me around. That's his job … yeah … he worked in the washing machine factory for 40 years, got a good pension, and we take vacations every year. Gotta get away. We'll be visitin' Crystal and Kenny a lot."

After breakfast, they drove back to Maggie's house and Eleanor chattered all the way, urging Richard and Maggie to visit them in Illinois.

Chapter 27

A month had passed since the wedding. One evening, Maggie came home to find a beat up truck in her driveway. When she opened her door, the truck door opened and three people tumbled out. It was Maggie's mother and father, and her brother, Joey.

For a moment, Maggie was speechless. Here was her family, whom she hadn't seen, or heard from, since she was ten years old, standing in her driveway!

"Hi there, Maggie girl," her father called, hurrying to hug her. "Just got news of Kenny's wedding so we missed it. Here's your mom, sweetie, and your brother, Joey."

Her mother, Constance Monahan, hugged her and shoved Joey forward.

"Hi, Maggie, long time no see!" Joey said, taking her hand.

"Come in, come in," Maggie said, and they all trooped in after her, throwing their coats on a chair in the foyer.

"Quite a place you got here, honey. You're a teacher, right? Kenny told us you owned this place … wow … got a maintenance guy, too, living next door. Kenny told us all about you getting this from that woman at Crosswell."

"Please sit down, and I'll make coffee. It's Friday, and I usually go to the grocery store on Saturday, but I've got bacon and eggs and fruit …"

Joey spoke up. "Great, I'm starvin'."

Constance followed Maggie into the kitchen.

"I'm not much for cookin' but I can give you a hand, Maggie."

"Thank you." Maggie could not bring herself to call this woman, who had abandoned her, Mother, let alone the more familiar Mama. She decided she wouldn't call her anything. The same with her father, Bill.

Maggie got out four plates, cups and saucers and set them on the kitchen table. She put on the coffee and took bacon and eggs from the fridge.

Constance was talking to her, but Maggie was in a daze. The words barely registered. Constance was saying as she placed the plates on the table, "Sorry, we didn't touch base with you, Maggie. Knew you were okay though. That nosy Perkins woman next door told me some old hag from Social Services came out and found you. We were comin' back, but I had a chance to sing at the Golden Arrow and I thought you'd be okay for a week or so. When we did get back, heard you were taken to that Crosswell place where someone would feed you and take care of you, send you to school 'til I got my big break. Joey, he's had it tough. I think Kenny's going to let him work at the club, if that snooty wife of his will let him. She's already laid down the law ... he works or he's out!"

The four ate their supper almost in silence. Maggie told them they could watch TV in the den while she cleaned up the kitchen. "You must be tired from traveling, so just relax. We'll visit awhile and then I'll show you where the bathroom and guest rooms are upstairs, when you want to turn in."

136

As she cleaned the kitchen, Maggie could hear laughter coming from the den. They must be having a good time. She felt like yelling at them, 'Why didn't you come back for me? I was your kid and only ten years old! You didn't even send a birthday card or a Christmas card, nothing until you show up on my doorstep.'

Maggie used the kitchen phone to call Richard.

"Guess who came to dinner."

"I have no idea!"

"My mother, my father, and my brother, Joey."

Richard sensed her frustration. "Maggie, it will be okay. Seems like we're always going to breakfast, but I'll come by about eight and we'll go over to the Blackhawk. There's a great buffet there, and we'll find out what their plans are."

Chapter 28

According to Crystal, Joey was working out okay at the club. Kenny insisted on calling the place 'my club'.

Crystal had designated Thursday nights as 'stew night' and supper was served regularly from six to nine. Crystal found a second-hand commercial dishwasher, which made cleanup a lot easier. Joey didn't mind loading the dishwasher, but flatly refused to scrub up the kitchen or do general cleaning. Joey called that 'woman's work'. However, he did enjoy working in the bar.

Joey tried to start a card game one evening about seven, but both Kenny and Crystal put the blocks on that. Kenny yelled at the top of his lungs, "Gambling is illegal in this state. Do you want this place shut down? Go get a job at the Indian reservation if you want to play cards for a living."

That was the end of the card game at the club, but Joey decided that Maggie's place would be as good as the club. On Fridays, he didn't have to be at Crystal and Kenny's until six, so Friday afternoons would work out just fine.

The first inkling that Maggie had about a card game in her house was when she came home one Friday afternoon about five-thirty to find beer cans on the kitchen table, overflowing ashtrays, plates in the sink and something that looked like potato chips and other snacks on the floor.

What a mess! Maggie went upstairs to her room

and changed clothes.

As she took the beer cans from the table to put them under the sink in her recycle trashcan, she had to stop and get a sack. The trashcan was overflowing!

Miss Cooper would never allow such a mess in her house, nor would she allow beer or cigarettes. Maggie muttered, "I have to talk to Joey. I can't have Miss Cooper's house smelling like beer, or cigarette butts on the floor either!" She sacked up the cans, washed off the table and opened the fridge door to take out leftover meatloaf for supper.

There were also two twelve-packs of Bud. A half-eaten opened pack of lunchmeat was on the second shelf, and a mustard jar that still had the knife in it. Maggie put the knife in the sink and opened a can of fruit to eat with her meatloaf. She kept celery and carrot sticks in the fridge. She poured a glass of skim milk, and sat down. She pulled up another kitchen chair and put up her feet. After standing most of the day in the classroom, putting up her feet was one of Maggie's little things she did for herself.

The following Friday, Maggie came home at four o'clock. The kitchen was just about the same as last week, the table littered with beer cans, ashes on the floor, ashtrays overflowing, and lunchmeat opened in the fridge. This Friday, there was only one twelve-pack.

She sighed, went upstairs to change, and on her way to her room, paused at Joey's door. He had left it half open. She pushed the door slightly. The bed was unmade, Joey's clothes were on the floor, and a tube of what looked like lipstick was on the dresser, along with a comb with a lot of red hair on it.

He must have a girlfriend, Maggie thought, as she closed the door partway, as Joey had left it. Well, the guy had to have friends. Miss Cooper would never approve of a young woman in a man's room, nor the beer, nor the cigarettes. Maggie cringed as she thought, I have to lay down some rules, but I shouldn't have to make rules for him. He's older. He's my big brother! One of them anyway.

Maggie ran some hot water in the sink, added the detergent, and started to clean up the kitchen. I'll call Richard. He'll know what to say and not hurt Joey's feelings. She walked to the phone in the living room. Two cushions were off the sofa, the coffee table was strewn with magazines that she had left neatly stacked when she finished them, and the blinds were crooked on the west window.

Maggie loved her living room just as Miss Cooper had furnished it. A Victorian type entertainment center housed a TV set; Queen Anne end tables with a matching coffee table bracketed the sofa. She could close the draperies and plantation blinds at night and leave them open during the day to let in the sunshine. She couldn't let Joey trash Miss Cooper's house. He doesn't care about anything. She walked to the phone and called Richard. He would know what to say to Joey.

Chapter 29

Maggie beckoned to Richard to follow her into the kitchen. She waved her hand over the kitchen table and over the floor.

"Richard, I know you don't like to hear about Miss Cooper's ideas, but I can't let Joey just wreck this duplex! The living room's a mess, too. I don't want to hurt Joey's feelings. He needs another month or two to save up enough to be on his own."

"Sit down, Maggie. How long has this been going on?"

"This is the second week. I think he brings a girl in, too. Four or five of his friends come every Friday for cards. I thought about leaving him a note, but then again, I thought it might have been a one-time occurrence. Miss Cooper would turn over in her grave if she knew this!"

"I'll help you clean up, Maggie, and we can talk about it. Then you're coming to my place. Believe it or not, I can whip up a meal if I have to! It's not a good idea to leave him a note. You have to tell him ... no drinking, no smoking. These are the house rules, your house rules. Just remember, Maggie, this is *your* house!"

"But he is my brother, Richard, and I need to help him get on his feet."

"But on your terms, not his! Let's say you bought this duplex, that it never belonged to Miss Cooper. Would you want ashes and spilled beer on the floor, food left opened in the fridge, the living room messy?"

"Of course not, but I didn't buy this place, Richard. It was given to me!"

"That it was, Maggie, that it was, but Miss Cooper expected you to take care of it. Otherwise, she wouldn't have left it to you, would she?"

"Probably not, but I still have to help him!"

"No, you don't, Maggie. You don't owe him a thing. You just *want* to help him, and that's okay, but on your terms. Get off early next Friday, better yet, get a substitute for Friday afternoon, and we'll surprise Joey's little card party."

"All right, but what will I say to Joey?"

"Maggie, I repeat. This is *your* house. You'll know what to say. You don't want any drinking or smoking in your house, but Joey can have his friends in for a game of cards and some refreshments with the condition that he leave the kitchen just as he found it. If you want to help him entertain, buy some soft drinks and crackers and stuff, maybe make some cookies the night before or something.

"Yes, I'll make cookies. I dread facing him. He's always so cheerful, calls me Mag, thanks me when I do his laundry ..."

"Whoa, Maggie! Laundry? He has as much time as you have. Show him where the laundry supplies are and how to dial the temperatures and the water level and he's all set."

"I think Mama did our laundry, but I can't remember too clearly. Mama had a friend who ironed her singing costumes. Maybe Daddy did the laundry.

142

No, the boys took clothes to the Laundromat down on Second Street, Daddy, too."

"Then Joey can go to the Laundromat, too."

Maggie hesitated. "Richard, Joey wants to borrow my car this coming Monday. He wants to go over to Bettendorf to see a friend. Kenny won't let him use his car. I think Crystal has been picking him up for work. Remember, Mama said he's been in trouble, DWI fines and things."

"Loaning him your car is not a good idea, Maggie. He could wreck it and possibly hurt someone if he drives and drinks. There's a bus to Bettendorf. He can take that and you can pick him up Monday evening when he gets back. I can look at the bus schedules. I'll be glad to take him to the bus."

"I don't think he's going to like that. Shall I talk to Kenny about the car? Shall I help Joey get one, or just buy a good used car for him to go back and forth to work and take little trips?"

"It's your money and your brother. Talk to Kenny. We can drop by the club tonight. Are things going well there?"

"Yes, Crystal told me they are doing fine. They won't have to borrow any money to keep open. Thanks for helping me clean up, Richard. I'll talk to Joey about the laundry tomorrow."

"Good. He's a big boy! Let's go and after supper, we can take a walk and catch a movie. I'll look in the paper and see what's playing. We'll drop by the club after the movie."

Maggie took out her door key, and she and

Richard left for his condo to enjoy hamburgers and a salad.

Chapter 30

When Maggie and Richard arrived at Kenny's Club, as Kenny was fond of calling his place, he waved them to a booth in the back and came over shortly.

"So, what's up, you two … things going okay with Joey? He's not the most ambitious guy on the planet."

Maggie did not hesitate. "Joey wants to play cards on Friday. He leaves my kitchen a mess, beer cans half full, food not covered in the fridge. I think he's also bringing a girl. The girl is okay, Kenny, but I don't like cigarette butts on the floor and ashes all over the place. He goes into the living room and leaves that a mess, too."

"Well, Maggie, darlin' sister, exactly whose house is it? Yours or Joey's?"

"Well, mine, but I don't want to hurt his feelings or make him feel he's not welcome. I just don't like to come home to a mess."

"Well, lay down the law. Use the ashtrays and empty them, wipe off the table, sweep the floor if necessary, put food back in the fridge. In short, Maggie, my love, tell him to leave the house as he found it. Is he looking for another place?"

"I don't know." Maggie folded and refolded her napkin. "He seems to like it at my place. I buy things for his breakfast and lunch. He comes to work about four, doesn't he?"

"Yeah," Kenny said. "I don't know about how

much work he does, but he comes in. He should be finding his own place. Why don't you give him a couple more months? He has to have a month's rent and a deposit of a month's rent around here. He should be on his feet by then. I pay him every Friday night. What does he do most weekends, Maggie?"

"He always borrows my car on Saturday night when he comes home from the club. On Sunday he sleeps."

"Well, that's typical," Kenny replied. "I'll get us something to drink. What do you want, Maggie?"

"Oh, just decaf coffee for me."

Richard thought a beer would be okay, so Kenny went to the bar and fixed the orders and brought them over.

"Look, Maggie, I know Joey's got this gamblin' thing in his blood. Got him into a lot of trouble over the years. I don't allow playin' cards for money. All kinds of things can happen over gamblin' debts."

"How will I stop him? I can't stay home every Friday afternoon."

"No, you can't. You'll just have to include that in your list of no-nos. Richard, what's your take on this?"

Richard took Maggie's hand. "It's as you say, Kenny. It's Maggie's house and she has to set the rules."

"Okay," Kenny said. "Maggie, you're too easy on him. Tell you what I'll do, Maggie. I'll talk to him when he comes in to work Monday night. I'll just sit down with him in my office and lay it out. He thinks he's on the gravy train; you'll let him stay as long as he wants. Why should he leave? He's got it made. High time little brother is on his own. Yeah, two months ought to do it. Tell you what, Maggie, like I say, I'll talk to him when he comes in Monday night for work. He thinks he's got it made, and well, he has, free room and board, use of your car, your phone. You're doin' his laundry. It's time to boot him out."

Maggie reached over and hugged Kenny. "I'm so glad you will talk to him, Kenny. I don't want to hurt his feelings. He's fun to be around and makes me laugh, but I don't know if it's good for him in the long run."

"No, it isn't, Maggie. We'll see how he reacts to our little talk."

Maggie and Richard left shortly after ten.

Chapter 31

Kenny lost no time when Joey arrived at work on Monday. "In the back office, kid. We need to talk."

"About what?" Joe muttered all the time he walked to the back.

"About Maggie and you messin' up her place ... leaving it like a pigpen when you and your pals are finished with your little card games on Friday."

"Oh, Maggie don't care. She's an okay gal."

"Yes, she does care, Joey, she just doesn't want to hurt your feelings. You know, ma told us how long she lived in that girls' school where everything was top notch. She hates messes ... and the old gal left her that duplex and that fancy furniture 'cause she knew Maggie would take care of it."

"Maggie lucked out, Kenny. It's okay for her to share with us. She set you up, didn't she? Gave you the money to start up this place."

"Yes, she did, but it's not 'gave' ... it's loaned. Crystal and me pay her every month, every first of the month on time."

"Ah, she wouldn't care if you missed a payment. Didn't the old girl leave her a pile of dough along with the house? And she and that boy friend of hers own a rental place somewhere ... rented it to a waitress with some kids."

"I never asked Maggie about the rental house. Crystal and me have enough of our own business to take care of. You shouldn't be playin' cards for money in her house and leaving her place a mess every

Friday. And you be damn careful with her car. She could lose her insurance if you had a few and hit somebody or worse."

"Oh, Kenny, I'm not going to do that. One more DUI and I'll lose my license for good. I know that."

"Well, get your own damn car. Save your money. You don't have any expenses. Save up enough to get you a used car and a small apartment near the club. Then you could walk to work and stop freeloading on Maggie."

"I've got expenses, Kenny."

"What expenses?"

"I've got to have a little fun ... work all week in your joint ... gotta buy the drinks on Friday and then me and Dolly got to have a good time Saturday night. You've got a woman, Kenny. Can't I have one?"

Kenny ignored Joey's whining. "Sure you can. Do like I did and marry her. Get an apartment and you can be together all the time."

"I don't want to get married. Don't want to be tied down. Besides all women are alike ... in the dark that is ... and I don't want a woman naggin' me to do stuff. I'm my own boss and I like it that way."

"That's fine, Joey, as long as you're payin' your way, but you ain't payin' your way when you're spongin' off Maggie."

"But she's loaded. I looked in her desk one day and her bank statement shows she's not starvin' ... and she's got over $5,000 in her checkin' account. I'll bet you and Crystal ain't got that much. Maggie's got a bunch of dough in a money market, too, a bunch."

"That's none of your business, Joey. Quit snoopin' like some old woman tryin' to find our Maggie's business. She trusts you, and you keep your fingers off her money."

"Oh, all right. I haven't asked her for any money, but I might ask her to float me a loan for a car."

"Earn your own damn car. You can save ... you haven't got any livin' expenses to speak of. Time to get to work and stay out of Maggie's desk."

They left Kenny's office and Joey began to wipe off tables. Kenny went to work behind the bar.

***

The next morning, Kenny called Richard at the hospital. He had never spoken to Richard on the phone and, when his assistant asked who was calling, he answered, "Kenny, Maggie's brother."

"Richard, phone for you," she called. "Maggie's brother."

The first words Richard said were, "Kenny, is Maggie okay?"

"Yeah, she's fine. It's about Joey. He's been looking through her desk. Told me how much Maggie had in her checkin' account. You'd better tip Maggie off and tell her to keep her money stuff somewhere else ... maybe over to your place. Would that be okay with you?"

"Sure," Richard answered. "I'll see Maggie tonight and tell her what you told me. Best to keep temptation out of Joey's way. He doesn't have any expenses. Maggie buys gas and feeds him and she doesn't charge him any rent. What does he do with the money you pay him?"

Kenny took a deep breath. "He's losing it gamblin'. I told him to save his money and buy a secondhand car. He wants Maggie to loan him the money ... no, I think he wants her to give it to him. He needs to earn the money. He's totaled two cars already and is on his second DUI. I don't know if Maggie will listen to me. She feels sorry for him, but she'll listen to you, won't she? She's your girl, isn't she?"

For a moment, there was complete silence. Richard had never stopped to define his feelings for Maggie, but he knew he couldn't let some no good, even if he were Maggie's brother, take advantage of her. "Yes, she's my girl. I'll talk to her tonight, Kenny. That's a good idea for her to leave her checkbook and financial stuff over at my place."

"Thanks, Richard. Gotta go. Look after Maggie. She's an okay gal, even if she is my sister."

After Kenny hung up, Richard turned to his assistant. "Cancel any appointments I have after 2:30. I'll be gone the rest of the afternoon."

Richard met Maggie at the school at three o'clock. She came hurrying out, her briefcase bulging with papers to correct. Richard tapped his horn lightly, opened the window, and called her.

"Hi, Maggie. Something came up and I need to talk to you. I'll follow you home."

Maggie stopped at his car. "Is Joey okay ... is it Kenny or Crystal?"

"They're all okay, but we need to talk about

Joey."

When they arrived at Maggie's place, she hurried up the sidewalk and unlocked the door, set her briefcase by the stairs and held her house keys in her hand.

"Sit down, Maggie, it's about Joey. Kenny called me at the hospital. Joey's been going through your desk and looking at your checkbook and your bank statements. If you let him stay here, you have to move them. Kenny suggested you leave them at my place."

"But why? Joey has never asked me for money. Kenny pays him every week. He told me he did."

"Kenny told me Joey has a gambling problem. If he can't pay his gambling debts and gets desperate, he'll ask you and tell you it's for something else. Or he might just try to steal it from you."

"Joey wouldn't steal from me, Richard. There's no need. Kenny would help him if he needed money."

"Kenny wouldn't help him to pay gambling debts, Maggie. For medical reasons, maybe. Kenny wants him to save his money and buy a secondhand car. He's had two DUIs and totaled the cars both times."

"I can't believe Joey would steal from me after I let him live here."

"When people get desperate, they do desperate things. You don't know what he does on the weekends … where he goes. If he's gambling, and Kenny thinks he is, and is losing, look out. It could be very bad business."

"All right. I'll get the bank statements and my checkbook."

"Get your box of checks, too, Maggie. Let's stop at the bank and tell them you'll pick up your statements."

Maggie went to the desk and opened the box of unused checks. "Richard, a book of checks is missing. Joey wouldn't forge my signature, would he?"

"I don't know. Order a new box and have them held at the bank. The bank can record the check numbers of the missing book and stop payment on any checks written."

"Oh, Richard, why would Joey think he needed to steal a book of my checks? If he asked me, I could let him have some money."

"I don't know. It's best to remove temptation from the house." He paused a minute, then stepped closer to her. "Kenny asked me something else."

"What did he ask you?"

"If you were my girl."

"Your girl? Why would he ask you that?"

"Because he knows I want to keep you from having anything bad happen to you. Joey getting into trouble would hurt you. I know that it would. You *are* my girl, Maggie. I just never told you."

He held her as she clutched her checkbook and the box of checks in her hand.

Chapter 32

The phone rang just as Maggie started to lock the front door. "I'd better answer it," she said. "It might be Kenny."

It was Kenny. He greeted her in his usual way. "Hi there, Maggie, I just called to let you know I found Joey an apartment. About two blocks from the club. It's not really an apartment … just a living room and bedroom. No kitchen, but that's okay because he can eat here. He can swing the rent, too."

Maggie hesitated a moment. "Kenny, a book of my checks is missing. Richard and I are going to the bank soon and order a new book. He says that the bank will stop payment on any checks written from the stolen book."

"Good idea. Talk to Joey when he comes in today about the apartment. If Joey gives you any flack, I'll talk to him. Listen, Maggie, talk to Richard about this, but I think you should get the locks changed now that Joey will have his own place. I'm going to advance him the first month's rent, and I'll take it out of his pay a little at a time."

"I don't think Joey will give me any flack," Maggie replied, "but thank you anyway."

Maggie and Richard drove to the bank together in Richard's car.

When they stopped at a traffic light, Richard reached over and put his hand on hers. "How long has Mr. Scott been the caretaker at your place, Maggie? You told me once, but I've forgotten."

"He was there when I came. He lived in the duplex before Miss Cooper died. She told me in her letter to me that he would always do the yard work, wash the outside windows, and things like that. Sometimes I don't see him for weeks at a time, but it's comforting to know he's right next door."

"You know, Maggie, he'll need to change his locks, too. Joey might figure he could access your place through Mr. Scott's place. But then again, if a thief wants to get in, sometimes a lock won't stop him."

"I'll call Mr. Scott when I get home," Maggie said. "He's always home by five. I think he volunteers at the Youth Center. Do you think I should tell Mr. Scott about Joey?"

"I think you must. Otherwise, he'll wonder why you're changing the locks at this time."

"All right. I'll just tell him Joey is moving out and that I think the locks ought to be changed. I could tell Mr. Scott I didn't approve of some of Joey's friends and would feel safer if the locks were changed."

"That's enough to tell him," Richard agreed.

When they walked into the main lobby of the bank, Maggie remembered Elaine, the first teller near the door. Elaine listened to Maggie's request for temporary checks, and filled out an order blank for new ones.

"We'll stop payment on any checks from the book that is missing, Maggie. No charge."

"Could I have my bank statements held at the

bank for the next few months?"

"Of course, Maggie, we hold them for people all the time. Statements are out by the tenth of each month and will be here waiting for you."

Maggie thanked her, put the temporary checks in her purse, and they went to Richard's house.

When they walked into the kitchen, Richard said, "I think it would be a good idea for you not to go to school tomorrow. Call in and tell them you need an emergency personal day. I take it you have a few coming, don't you?"

"I've never asked for personal days off, Richard. No sick days this semester, either."

"Good. Again, you need to change the locks and have new keys made. No telling what kind of people Joey is running around with. This girlfriend of his, for example. She may have acquaintances you wouldn't want in your home."

"Oh, Richard, I never thought I'd have to change the locks on my own brother. Had he asked me, I would have given him money."

"True, Maggie, but you don't know how deeply in debt he is. Otherwise, he wouldn't have stolen your book of checks and your last bank statement. When you owe gambling debts, the people holding the debt are pretty rough sometimes. Let's put your checks in my desk drawer. The desk has a lock, which I've never used, but it will come in handy."

They drove to the hardware store on Ripley Street. Richard wasn't sure he could change the locks and align them properly, so the clerk at the hardware store gave them the name of a locksmith.

At Maggie's house, she called the locksmith, who told her he would come promptly at nine the next morning.

"Let's get your legal papers, anything to do with your inheritance, and take them to my house," Richard said. "I'll have a duplicate key made to the desk, and I'll get a duplicate key for my house so you can come in when you need to."

"All right, Richard, but I still don't feel right about changing the locks and removing my papers."

"I know, Maggie. I don't have a brother, but I'm sure I'd feel the same way."

"Can we keep the police out of this? I thought about asking them to drive by a time or two when I'm at school next week, but I'd have to tell them why, wouldn't I?"

"I think so, but why don't you wait and see what happens next week. Tell your neighbor what the deal is and ask him to keep an eye on your apartment. And we should go by the club and tell Kenny. He needs to be aware that Joey has taken off with your pad of checks and that we've been to the bank."

The next morning, Maggie called the school at seven-thirty. Mr. Simmons, the assistant principal, answered.

"Mr. Simmons, I need a personal day today, for a family emergency. I hope I'm calling early enough for you to get a sub."

"You are, Maggie. I hope you get things resolved."

"Thank you, Mr. Simmons."

Maggie made coffee and found a Kraft envelope in the bottom drawer of her desk. She put the copy of Miss Cooper's will, the deed to the property, and her cancelled checks in the envelope, then she went upstairs to make her bed and clean the bathroom.

Richard called at nine. The locksmith had just come and had started removing the lock on the front door.

"Good morning, Richard, the locksmith is here. He's going to change the locks on the back and side doors, too. I haven't talked with Mr. Scott yet, but I will."

"Good. Did you get your personal day?"

"Yes, Mr. Simmons said I'd called early enough. Sometimes it's a hassle to get a sub on short notice."

"I took the day off, too. What do you think of going over to Kenny's and filling him in?"

"Yes, I think we should. As soon as the locksmith is finished, I'll be over. Thank you, Richard. I'm calmer now and I can think better. I'll see you in about an hour.

Chapter 33

Richard had new keys made for his apartment before Maggie got there. When she rang the doorbell, he beckoned her inside.

"Give me your key ring, Maggie. Here are the two keys you'll need. This small one is to the desk and the round headed key is to the front door." He snapped them on Maggie's key ring and they walked into the kitchen.

"Let's have coffee, Maggie. We need to talk about Joey and about us."

"Us?"

"Yeah, us. I want to marry you. I want to take care of you. I worry about you since this whole business of Joey and his ransacking your place started. I don't think you're safe in your own home with Joey around with that girlfriend of his." He placed his hand over hers. "But more importantly, Maggie, I love you. I want to spend the rest of my life with you."

She closed her gaping mouth. Marriage? She hadn't given it more than a passing thought in her entire life. "Oh, Richard, you've done so much for me ... when I was sick ... Julie's apartment and her kids ... this whole business with my family showing up. You've been there for Kenny and Crystal." She took a deep breath. "But I don't think I'm ready to get married. I've not even been teaching a year. I'm not sure if I ever have been on my own, to become what Miss Cooper wanted me to be. She didn't know that my family would show up after all these years. I feel I need to work awhile and prove to myself that I can truly support myself. I remember as if it were yesterday when I told her how hungry I was when I was little and that sometimes Daddy didn't have the rent money and we were cold. That's why she told me I should be able to support myself so I would never have to worry about being hungry again." Her voice trailed to a whisper as she took another sip of coffee.

"Look, Maggie," Richard said. "It's not like Miss Cooper is here looking over your shoulder, examining everything you do. So far, I think you've done okay with the bank sending you to work at the hospital, getting back into teaching, helping Kenny get on his feet. Now let's talk about our wedding. We could have a small service and get the minister who preached Miss Cooper's funeral to perform the service. I'd like to invite my secretary and associates at the hospital and, of course, Crystal and her folks and your parents and Mr. Scott, yeah, and that banker guy and your lawyer. Hey, this list is getting to be a crowd!"

Maggie looked at him thoughtfully. He was going much too fast for her. "I just don't know if I'm cut out for marriage. Miss Cooper never married."

"No, she didn't, Maggie, but look at the kids she gave a good start in life, including you! I know she'd want you to be happy."

"But, Richard, I feel I haven't lived up to what she expected of me, to be able to live on my own."

"You're paying your bills with your earnings, aren't you? You save some of your salary, and you help people. I think you have lived up to her expectations and then some. You've certainly lived up to mine. I think you're great! Tell you what. We'll name our first girl Rachel, the second one Rebecca, and the first boy will be Cooper!"

"Aren't you rushing things? We have a problem with Joey."

He eyed her for a moment. "Okay, Maggie, we'll set aside the subject of marriage, but only temporarily, mind you! I want to help you with Joey, but let him struggle a bit with his gambling problem. I think, eventually, he'll come to realize he can't make a living by gambling. Heck, Maggie, you might have to practice tough love!"

"But how? I can't I can't just ignore him!"

"I know you can't, Maggie, but you'll have to make him face his problem."

"Maybe Kenny and I should talk to him, together. It seems weird for me to say this, but I don't really know Joey, but I think Kenny does. Do you think Kenny can help him?"

"Only if he wants to help himself. If Joey thinks gambling is an easy way to make a living, then I'm afraid he's going to have tough sailing. He must learn by experience that gambling isn't a sure way of making a living. I don't want to scare you, Maggie, but I think Joey's mixed up with some bad people who will stop at nothing to get the money he owes them."

"Oh, Richard, do you think they'll hurt him?"

"Yes, I do and so does Kenny."

"Oh, merciful heaven! Let's go talk to Kenny."

"All right, but let's wait 'til afternoon. We'll see

if Joey comes back to the house and tries to break in after we changed the locks, or if his girlfriend does. Let's go over and park where we can see the duplex, then whether anything happens or not, we'll go to Kenny's place and let him know. After that, we'll talk some more about getting married."

"All right, Richard. It's just that I'm not sure I've earned my way yet, and until I do, I don't want to get married. I do love you, though." That remark surprised her and she hurried over it. When did she start loving him, not just depending on him as a friend? "Let's go over to the duplex and wait."

They left his condo in Richard's car.

Chapter 34

That evening, Maggie and Richard sat in the alley where they had a good view of the back of Maggie's duplex. The back of the garage was right on the alley between Lombard and Kirkwood running east and west. Maggie and Richard were in the alley running north and south.

They heard the clock on the Kirkwood Memorial building chime at six o'clock.

"How much longer shall we wait, Richard?" Maggie looked at her watch. The time agreed with the big clock.

"Maybe another half an hour. It will be dark then. Do you see any lights on in Mr. Scott's place?"

Maggie answered, "Look at that basement window. I think he leaves a light on all night. No, I think he has it on a timer. I came in from Crosswell one night about midnight and it was still on. The front porch is on a sensor and comes on when you come to the bottom step."

"I don't think anyone will break in at the front," Richard said. "But let's keep an eye on the back of the house."

Fifteen minutes later, they saw three people walking toward the house.

"Look, Maggie, there's three of them, two men and a girl. You can see her pony tail. Listen ..." Richard touched the button and the window rolled down silently. "You can hear her boots. The men must be wearing sneakers."

"What shall we do, Richard? Call the police?"

"You stay in the car, Maggie, and I'll go over to the pay phone on Kirkwood. I'll be right back."

Richard called the police from a telephone booth at Kirkwood and Vine. The desk cop said he would send someone immediately. Richard returned to the car, where Maggie was watching the house.

"They had a key, Richard."

"Joey must have had one made. I hope to God one of them isn't Joey. Burglary is a criminal offense and he could get sent up." Richard looked at his watch. It was 6:20.

The police entered the property from the alley, then each one stood on either side of the duplex. They wore street clothes.

Neither Richard nor Maggie said a word. After what seemed like an eternity to them, the trio came out the back door. The girl had a small suitcase with her. The men didn't have anything in their hands.

The three intruders got to the middle of the walk, when the two detectives came up behind them and told them to stop. The one on the right flashed his badge, the other a plain police issue handgun.

"I'll take this," the one officer said to the girl while the other officer expertly handcuffed all three of them and pushed them to the waiting police car. They called to Maggie and Richard. "Come down to the Main Street Station. You'll need to press charges."

"Okay," Richard said, as he walked to the police car. He did not recognize the two men, but he did remember the girl. He had seen her coming out of

164

Maggie's duplex with Joey.

Richard waved to the officers, and he and Maggie followed them to the Main Street station.

The detective had dumped the contents of the bag onto a table. Maggie identified the watch that Miss Cooper had given to her, a string of pearls, a small pendant, a man's fob watch, a pair of diamond earrings and a ruby necklace, all from Maggie's jewelry box that Miss Cooper had left her.

The three burglars were standing in handcuffs. The desk sergeant asked Maggie, "Recognize these three?"

She answered in a firm voice. "The girl. She has been in my home several times. I have never seen the men."

The officer smiled at Maggie. "We'll just need to take a picture of your jewelry then you can take everything home."

With that, the officer pressed a buzzer on the desk and a uniformed policeman came and took the three to the cell block.

"Miss Monahan, we'll notify you when we schedule an arraignment. Good night."

Maggie and Richard left the police station and went to the duplex. Only the bedroom had been entered. The top drawer of the dresser was open. Maggie closed it.

"Richard, we had the locks changed. The police didn't find a key on them, so how did they get in?"

"Probably jimmied the lock. I think he used some sort of tool. He got in right away."

"Do you think they were friends of Joey's?"

"No, I think they were fences … people who buy stolen stuff. I think Joey owes somebody a lot of money. This was probably the girl's idea. She figured if she stole the stuff, she could sell it to someone and get the money for Joey. Chances are he doesn't know anything about the burglary. Let's go over to Kenny's place. Joey might be working or Kenny might know where he is.

"That's a good idea, Richard. Oh, I hope Joey isn't in on this. I couldn't bear for him to be in prison!"

"Don't borrow trouble," Richard cautioned. "I hope Joey doesn't know anything about this either. We have to get him out of this mess. We may have to loan him the money to get him free of them."

"Oh, Richard, I would give him the money. Let him stay with me forever, if I have to. Anything!"

"Whoa, Maggie, my darling, not so fast. That's not the way to get him on his feet. He needs to take responsibility for his actions. Kenny and both of us will help him figure out the best thing to do."

Maggie's thoughts were jumbled with fear, happiness that Joey wasn't doing the robbing, and how they could get him on the right path. She and Richard drove in silence the rest of the way to Kenny's place.

Chapter 35

When Richard and Maggie arrived at Kenny's club, she was so happy to see Joey wiping down the bar that she ran over and hugged him.

"Hey, Maggie, what's up? I'm glad to see you, too."

"Oh, Joey, the police just arrested that girl who has been coming to my house. She was with two men I didn't know. They broke into my house. Oh, Joey, I'm so glad you weren't there!"

Joey sat down on the bar stool. "Spike and two guys? The police came?"

Richard sat down beside Joey and looked him straight in the eyes. "You're lucky you were working. Your girlfriend was taking off with Maggie's jewelry. Some of the expensive stuff she got from Miss Cooper."

Kenny came over and stood by them. "Look, Joey, you've got to get rid of that girl. She's no good. She probably wanted to sell the stuff to get you out of hock! Whose idea was that, not yours, I hope."

Joey wiped his hands on the towel he was holding. "Of course, it wasn't my idea ... of all the dumb things to do and get caught at that!"

Kenny put his hand on Joey's shoulder. "How much are you into with this gamblin' bunch, Joey? No lies. Just the straight goods ... must be a bundle to get this girl to rob Maggie."

"I didn't tell her to rob Maggie, for God's sake. I just took Maggie's checkbook in case they had me to the wall."

Maggie cringed when Joey admitted the theft. She had resisted the idea that he would steal from her, but, on the other hand, now she wouldn't have to ask him about it.

Kenny asked again. "How much?"

"About two thousand."

"Two thousand! And just how soon do they want their money?"

Joey swallowed, paused, and then said, "They wanted it yesterday."

"Yesterday! And exactly who are they?"

"The guys I play cards with on Sunday night."

"What guys?"

"Just guys."

"Well, while your girlfriend explains all this to the cops, you are going to sign a Note," Kenny said. "I'm going to loan, get this *loan* you the money to bail you out, but it's the last time. Maggie, you stay here with Joey. Crystal's upstairs in the apartment. If Joey tries to leave, go get her, and she'll run him down. Richard, want to come with me?"

"You bet. Maggie, stay here and when we get back we'll all figure out something."

"Oh, Richard, Kenny can't afford to loan him the money. I'll just give it to him, then it will all go away."

Kenny walked over to where Maggie was standing and took her hand. "No, Maggie, we're, that means you and me, aren't giving our brother anything. He's goin' to earn it. For once, he's goin' to stand on his own two feet and get himself out of this mess. It's the last time I'm doing it. The next time, he can rot in jail or get his legs broken."

Broken legs? The thought hurt Maggie, but she agreed. "All right, Kenny. Are you sure you have enough?"

"Yes, we do. We've been building up the business. Our brother is going to work every night until he pays off the two thou. If he doesn't, he's out of here and on his own. I've had it with him."

Richard and Kenny went into Kenny's office.

Maggie sat by Joey at the bar. "Joey, is this girl … is she close … are you engaged to marry her?"

"Engaged! Good God, no, Maggie. Guys don't marry girls like Spike. She's okay to go to bed with and hang around with … besides I'm not marrying anybody. I don't trust women. Look at Ma … traipsing all over the country with Dad following her around like a hound dog, not giving a damn whether we have anything to eat or not. Look how she left you and you wound up in that damn school. Oh, I know, the old gal left you loaded, but she wasn't your Mama."

"Yes, she was, in everything that mattered." Maggie changed the subject. "Why do you gamble, Joey?"

"I don't know, Maggie. I want to live my own way … do my own thing … I don't want to work for anybody. I want to be my own boss … so, I gamble for the money, I guess."

"What money, Joey?"

His tone was belligerent. "Sometimes I win."

"I don't know how to help you, but I do know one thing. I don't want you beat up by thugs or go to jail." She hugged him and went to the restroom.

Joey was still sitting at the bar when Kenny came back. He wasted no words.

"Come on, Joey, you're taking us to your pals, paying them off, and then right back here and get to work. It's your last chance, Joey, take it or leave it."

Before the three left, Kenny called upstairs to Crystal. "Honey, come down and stay with Maggie. Richard, Joey and I will be gone about an hour."

The three of them left. Crystal came downstairs and made coffee for Maggie.

When the men left, Maggie began to cry. Crystal put her arm around her. "It's going to be okay, Maggie. Joey's not a bad kid … mostly lazy. I think Kenny will straighten him out this time."

"But what if Joey gets in with those awful people again?"

"I don't think he will, Maggie. I think he's scared. Kenny would let him go to jail, or whatever, if he gets in with this bad bunch again. Let's drink our coffee while we're waiting for them to come back."

Chapter 36

Kenny drove his pick-up to downtown Davenport. Joey sat beside him and Richard sat in the back seat of the spacious cab.

Joey broke the silence. "It's in the Kaul Building ... seventh floor ... 702."

"You play cards in an office building?" The question sounded as if Kenny couldn't believe that Joey would play cards on a Sunday night in an office building.

"Yeah. There're games goin' on in an office down the hall, too. I think a cop plays sometimes. That's why they don't get pinched for gamblin'." Joey started to light a cigarette when Kenny said, "No smokes, Joey. Crystal don't like cigarette smoke. She drives the truck a lot to pick up supplies."

"Well, okay. We can park right across the street. I can get in the front door. They gave me the combination to get in."

Kenny and Richard watched as Joey punched in the numbers on a panel by the door. When he was finished, the door opened and they took the elevator to the seventh floor.

Joey knocked twice and a man in a gray suit let them in. "Come to pay up, Joey?"

"Yeah. Where's Fred? I gotta see Fred."

The man who had let them in beckoned them to an inner office. Four men were playing cards at a round table.

Joe spoke to the one called Fred. "My brother

gave me the money I owe you. This here's Kenny." Joey stepped back as Kenny shook hands with Fred.

"This is the last time I'm bailin' Joey out of these card games. Any more and he's on his own. I'd suggest that you guys stop inviting him."

Fred had sat down and was picking up his hand of cards. "Well, now, Kenny, is it? Joey here is a big boy and he's gotta do his own thing."

"Well, that may be so, but you're goin' to whistle for your money if he loses any more money."

"Oh, no, we won't whistle … he'll pay! We have ways of getting guys like him to pay up. Some ain't so pleasant, but we always get our money."

Kenny glared at Joey. "See this money, Joey? This is the last time you get it, the *last* time!" He pulled out the $2,000 and threw it on the table in front of Fred.

Fred picked up the money and stuffed it into his pants pocket. "Nice meetin' you, Kenny, thanks for the money … until next time … Joey boy, he'll be back … brother or no brother!"

"Don't count on it," Kenny said, opening the door and shoving Joey out before him. Richard followed and they walked down the hall to the elevator.

As they got in Kenny's pick-up, he looked at Richard. "Is it okay if we drop you off at the bar? You can take Maggie home. Joey and I are going to talk this gamblin' thing out."

"Sure. Why don't you and Joey talk at my place? Here's the key. Maggie and I will hang out at

172

the bar for half an hour or so and then come over."

"Okay, Richard, and thanks."

Kenny dropped Richard at the bar and drove over to Richard's condo, thoughts of what he would say to Joey trying to find some semblance of sense. He was still furious and didn't trust himself to talk to Joey on the way over there.

When Richard joined Maggie, who was sitting with Crystal, she started to ask him how Joey was, but instead burst into tears.

Richard gathered her into his arms and patted her on her back. "It's okay, Maggie, it's going to be okay. I think this time Kenny will get through to Joey. It's happened a few times before, hasn't it, Crystal?"

"Yeah. Kenny told me about the times he bailed him out of a gamblin' fix."

"We're going to stay here for about half an hour, Crystal. Kenny took Joey to my place. It might be a good idea for Joey to stay with me a week or so, so those goons won't be bumping into him. They think he'll come back and gamble some more."

"Sure, Richard. I'm going upstairs. When you and Maggie get ready to leave, holler up and I'll come down. Kenny closed the place for the evening. He didn't know what was coming up with Joey."

"Thanks, Crystal. Let's sit down, Maggie." He held her hands and neither of them spoke for a few minutes. Richard broke the silence.

"Look, Maggie, I don't like you being so upset. I don't think I ever saw you cry before, except that day in the hospital when you told me you wanted to go back to teaching. Let's get married … maybe next week … I want to take care of you. I love you, Maggie. Forget about proving anything to Miss Cooper's memory. You just being you is enough! Let's tell Crystal and when we go to my place, we'll tell the boys … okay, Maggie?"

"What about Joey? Who will help him? Kenny won't anymore."

"We'll all help him, Maggie, give him a fair chance. I'll see if he's interested in work at the hospital. Does he have any hobbies? What does he like to do besides gamble?"

"I don't know, Richard. I really don't."

"Kenny and I will talk to him when we get back to my place. We'll figure out something, then we'll get married in two weeks. Okay, Maggie?"

She gazed into his eyes for a long moment. She certainly wanted to get married, and she already loved this man who was also her best friend. She nodded. "Yes."

Richard gently squeezed her hands. "We'll ask your Mom and Dad and a few people at the hospital … Mr. Scott and Crystal's parents … that's people enough … and Julie and her kids …"

"And Mr. Dawson and Mr. Charlesworth at the bank?"

"Okay, them, too. Let's go, Maggie, and tell Kenny and Joey!"

Richard called to Crystal. When she came downstairs, he said, "We're getting married in two weeks, Crystal. Get a hold of your Mom and Dad."

"I'm so happy for you both!" Crystal gave them each a big hug, kissed Maggie on her cheek and opened the door for them.

Chapter 37

Joey and Kenny were sitting in Richard's living room. Joey was putting out a cigarette.

Richard greeted them. "Let's have a drink. Maggie and I have some great news. A small glass of sherry won't hurt you, Maggie." Richard went to a small bar between the living room and dining area and took out a bottle of Scotch and a bottle of wine. He poured three tumblers of Scotch and a small glass of wine.

"Maggie and I are getting married in two weeks. You're all invited, of course. The ceremony will be in the Methodist Chapel, next to the hospital. We'll let you know the time."

Kenny and Joey shook hands with Richard and kissed Maggie. "Welcome to the family," Kenny said.

Joey added, "Yeah, welcome to the family. I mean it. You're okay, Richard, and Maggie … you're just Maggie." Both the brothers hugged her.

Maggie and Richard sat on the loveseat. He said, "Did you and Kenny work things out, Joey?"

"Yeah, if it's okay with you, Kenny thinks I should stay here a couple of weeks or so. Those goons don't know where you live."

"Sure, it's okay, Joey. How would you like to work for the hospital?"

"I don't like being around sick people. I don't want to scrub floors and clean up messes, either," Joey answered, his voice bordering on rudeness.

Richard thought, 'spoiled brat', but answered

calmly enough, "No, I didn't think you would. But Old Man Jaffee just retired from Maintenance and Mr. Carson needs a new apprentice. He'll train you and you'll start at Maintenance Tech entry wages. Maintenance assistants, they call people starting out in maintenance. They fix all kinds of things, Joey, like boilers, electrical equipment, IV connections, oxygen tanks and the like. It's specialized work. When you're done with training under Carson, the hospital will send you to school for classes and you'll come out with electrician's and plumber's licenses. Do you think you would like that?"

Joey didn't answer for a minute or so. He was slowly thinking about Richard's offer ... a chance to be something ... good money in it and maybe ... just maybe he would make it this time. He knew Kenny was through helping him.

His voice was firm when he answered. "Yeah, I'd like to try it. I'm not getting anywhere bussing dishes, sweeping floors and wiping down the bar at Kenny's place."

"No, you're not," Kenny agreed. "This is a break for you."

Maggie put her glass down on the coffee table. "When Richard and I are married, you can stay at the duplex when you think you're ready. In the meantime, I will leave it vacant and Mr. Scott can look after it until you want to move in."

"That's generous of you, Maggie, but Joey doesn't need to worry about housing, with the maintenance job. The hospital has two houses on the hospital grounds, which it rents to maintenance employees. Mr. Jaffee moved out last month. They have the houses there because most of the time Maintenance is on call."

"Are you sure the hospital will give me a job, Richard? I don't know how to fix anything, except maybe when a car breaks down. Even then, half the time I have to take it into the shop."

"Yes, the hospital will give you a job, Joey. I talked to Mr. Carson yesterday. Now, let's talk about the wedding. Kenny, we need your Mom and Dad and Crystal's Mom and Dad. Anybody special you want to invite, Joey?"

"I can't think of anybody right now, but maybe I'll find me a cute nurse someday."

"Maybe you will, Joey. Kenny, will you run Maggie home? Joey can stay here tonight in the guest room."

"Sure, Richard, I'll be glad to run Maggie home. After all, she's my favorite sister!"

As Kenny and Maggie drove to her duplex, Kenny told her how happy he was for her and that now she wouldn't be alone.

Joey was still on Maggie's mind. "Do you think Joey will stay away from gambling, Kenny?"

"He knows this is his last chance. It's great of Richard to find him a job. Your Richard is an okay guy! And, who knows, with a steady job and housing Joey might find himself a nice girl like you and Crystal … you two are the only nice girls I know … and then he'll settle down, get married and have some kids."

"I hope so, Kenny."

Kenny hugged her again when they stopped at her front door.

Maggie went upstairs, knowing that she would get a good night's sleep now that Joey was on the right track. Her last thought, before she drifted off, was 'what in the world will I wear to my wedding!"

Chapter 38

Maggie needn't have worried. The following day, Crystal took her to the Bridal Boutique on Kirkland Boulevard and they found a dress Maggie liked. It had a small train, beaded bodice and long tight sleeves. Crystal also helped her find shoes and talked her into a half veil.

"You'll look smashing, Maggie, all that white with your black hair, and I'd bet the club that you're a virgin. You, of all people, should wear white. You'll take Richard's breath away. If your Mom doesn't make it in time, Mom and I will help you get ready. Your folks have to come from Illinois, right?"

"That's right. Crystal, I know Mom and Dad don't have the money, so I want to pay for my wedding. Richard will pay for the reception."

Crystal interrupted her. "No, let Richard pay for the rehearsal dinner ... the groom usually does ... and Kenny and me will pay for the reception after the ceremony." Her eyes were shining as she rattled off the wedding plans.

"It's so much expense, Crystal! Can't we just get married and all of us go to dinner?"

"No, kiddo, you only get married once ... hopefully ... then after the reception, Richard will whisk you off!"

"Whisk me off?"

"Sure, Maggie, on your honeymoon. You don't think he's going to work the next day, do you? You've got to ask for a month's leave of absence from school.

180

You'll probably live in Richard's condo until you build your own house."

"We don't need a house, do we, Crystal? Richard's got a condo and I've got the duplex Miss Cooper left me."

"He'll want you to have your own house, Maggie, where you fix it and decorate it. You'll have fun furnishing it. I had fun fixing up the apartment over the club. You had fun fixing up that rental place for Julie, didn't you?"

"But that was different."

"You picked out the colors and stuff, didn't you? Weren't you painting when you got sick and Richard took you to the hospital?"

"Well, yes."

"You'll see. It will be fun. When Kenny and me have kids, we're getting a house, with a yard and stuff."

In the next week, Crystal arranged for all the relatives to come and made reservations in the Kirkwood Hotel for them.

Kenny and Joey got new suits.

Richard invited his staff at the hospital, and Bertha from Medical Records. Maggie invited Mr. Scott, Julie and two of the teachers at her school. She dropped notes to her lawyer and banker. There was no time for engraved invitations, Maggie thought.

***

The Wesleyan Chapel was on the East end of the hospital. Richard made arrangements with the Reverend Ray Barnett to conduct the service. The

181

ceremony began promptly at four o'clock on the third Saturday of the month.

Richard wore a pin stripe suit with a gray tie.

When the organist started to play the familiar strains of "Here Comes the Bride," Maggie walked down the center aisle on her father's arm. Margaret Saville Monahan and Dr. Richard Allen spoke their vows in less than ten minutes. After a brief prayer, the group left the Chapel for the Blackhawk Hotel, where the reception was held.

The party broke up at about eight, and Richard and Maggie took the elevator to the Bridal Suite on the ninth floor.

"Forever," Richard said, holding her close before he inserted the key. "Everything will be okay. You, me, Joey, Crystal and Kenny. You're all my family now." He lifted her face. "The best is that you're my wife. We're going to live, as the fairy tales say, 'happily ever after'."

As Richard unbuttoned her wedding dress, Maggie was sure Miss Cooper was smiling.

The End

Other Books by Opal M. Snyder

From Opal to Her Children

Enjoy Other Fine Books from Righter Publishing Company

Thrillers, detective stories, short story collections, children's books, inspirational works, poetry collections, family histories, science fiction, romance, literary fiction, local histories, personal memoirs and self-help.

Go to www.righterbooks.com

28626646R00105

Made in the USA
Charleston, SC
17 April 2014